"You can't

Mick concentrated on K
She didn't appear to be

"Let's go to my place and talk," he suggested.

Kelly nodded. She hadn't spoken since telling him....
Perhaps she'd gone into shock.

The drive to his house took less than five minutes.

"I understand that you must feel terrible about my
brother," he told her.

And he did. His journalistic training was too ingrained
for him not to see both sides of the story. Despite
his grief, he knew that Kelly had tried to defuse his
brother's fear, speaking to him calmly and gently. But
his brother had been too worked up. He'd cocked the
trigger of his handgun and that was it. Kelly had aimed,
fired...

"Don't think it's guilt behind my suggestion," Kelly said
now. "Mick, I genuinely care about those children. I
would do anything to help them. Anything."

Something in him wanted to give her whatever she
asked for. And, face it, she was offering him a solution
to his own dilemma. "How will you feel in a year, or two,
or ten? Kelly, I'm not interested in a temporary fix
here."

"I understand that. I do."

In the small, bookshelf-lined room, her words echoed
like a marriage vow....

Dear Reader,

"Shooting to kill is an officer's nightmare." This is the headline that caught my eye a few years ago when I was reading the *Calgary Herald* at my breakfast table. Years of Westerns, cop shows and mystery novels had ingrained in me the simple maxim that good guys shoot bad guys. But I had never before contemplated the complex dilemma an officer faces when making the choice to pull the trigger and end another life.

That morning the seed for A *Convenient Proposal* was planted. I knew I wanted to write a story about a cop who responds strictly by the book in a dangerous situation, then reacts like a sensitive human being in the months that follow. The cop is Kelly Shannon, the youngest of the three Shannon sisters.

If you read the first book of this trilogy, A *Second-Chance Proposal*, you may have wondered what Kelly was doing during her lengthy, unexplained absences from the Larch Lodge Bed and Breakfast near the end of the story. She wasn't at work—she'd been suspended, remember?—and she certainly wasn't out having fun.

Now I invite you to find out. To dive into Kelly's story and meet the children and the man who will change her life forever.

Sincerely,

C.J. Carmichael

P.S. I'd love to hear from you. Please send mail to the following Canadian address: #1754-246 Stewart Green, S.W., Calgary, Alberta, Canada T3H 3C8. Or send e-mail to: cjcarmichael@shaw.ca. For more information visit: www.cjcarmichael.com.

A Convenient Proposal
C.J. Carmichael

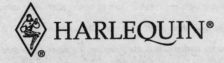

HARLEQUIN®

TORONTO • NEW YORK • LONDON
AMSTERDAM • PARIS • SYDNEY • HAMBURG
STOCKHOLM • ATHENS • TOKYO • MILAN • MADRID
PRAGUE • WARSAW • BUDAPEST • AUCKLAND

ISBN 0-373-71044-5

A CONVENIENT PROPOSAL

This trilogy is dedicated to my editors,
Beverley Sotolov and Paula Eykelhof,
with my thanks and affection.

ACKNOWLEDGMENTS

Thanks to those who assisted me in my research, in
particular Corporal Patrick Webb of the RCMP in Calgary,
Constable Barry Beales of the RCMP Canmore Detachment
and Lynn Martel, a reporter with the *Canmore Leader*.

PROLOGUE

SHE COULDN'T STOP SHAKING as she stared at the gun—her own Smith & Wesson—in a carefully labeled plastic bag. The weapon was Crown evidence; she wouldn't see it again for months.

On second thought, make that ever.

"You'd better sit down, Kelly."

"What?" RCMP officer Kelly Shannon looked from the .38 to the familiar face of her commanding officer, Staff Sergeant Springer.

That brief thought of her future, of there being moments, days, years that would follow, made her so damn weary. All she wanted was to curl up on the rain-dampened ground and be left alone. But Springer had stuck by her side since he'd arrived at the Thunder Bar M forty minutes ago.

"Let me take you to your car. You need to get off your feet."

If Kelly hadn't already understood the gravity of the situation, the staff sergeant's consideration and gentle tone would have tipped her off.

"I'm fine." She tried to protest, but large, well-muscled Springer put a hand to her elbow and courteously led the way to her patrol car. She noted her driver's-side door was still open, from that instant when she'd leaped out—galvanized by the sight of Danny Mizzoni holding a gun to her sister's head.

Springer settled her in the passenger side of the car, then checked his watch. "Backup from Calgary should be here shortly."

Kelly leaned against the headrest and closed her eyes briefly. Sitting wasn't such a bad idea. Her trembling was getting worse. Springer must have noticed, too, because he found a blanket and settled it over her lap.

"Thanks." She knew this calm wouldn't last long. Once the officers from Ident and the Major Crimes Unit arrived, there would be hours'—if not days'—worth of work to be done. She'd seen it before.

Homicides were rare in the rustic mountain community of Canmore, Alberta, but two-and-a-half years ago a young girl, Jilly Beckett, had been shot dead on this very property. Kelly had worked on that case.

But she wouldn't be working on this one.

"Someone from MAP will be here shortly, too." Springer patted her shoulder.

The representative from the Member Assistance Program would guide her through the next few hours. She would be suspended from duty, of course. There would be an investigation. Springer had already notified her of her rights. At some point she would need to hire a lawyer.

Anxiety set off another spasm of trembling. Kelly filled her lungs with air, then groped for the badge she'd always worn so proudly. Being a member of the Royal Canadian Mounted Police meant carrying on a tradition of honor. A tradition of which she was no longer worthy.

"I suppose you'll want this," she said, fumbling with the catch.

Springer put a hand on her shoulder and squeezed. "That isn't necessary, Kelly. Keep it. You're still one of us."

The wail of approaching sirens crescendoed with the rumbling of tires on gravel as the squad cars from Calgary arrived. Kelly watched them stream onto Thunder Bar M land. They lined up behind the ambulance, where the paramedics were standing by the open back doors and watching calmly, knowing it would still be some time before the coroner gave them permission to move the body.

Car doors and voices slammed into the afternoon quiet. Springer's hand tightened on her shoulder. She would soon be taken to the station, while these men and women worked at recording the details of the crime scene, collecting and cataloguing every shred of potential evidence.

How Dylan must hate this, she thought—having his land overrun with police and emergency workers. She wondered about her sister Cathleen, and hoped she was recovering from the shock of having Danny Mizzoni's gun held to her head. Dylan and Cathleen were out by the creek now. Sharon, Danny's wife—widow—and two kids, were in the kitchen with Danny's brother.

Thinking of those innocent bystanders, Kelly couldn't hold back a groan. Their pain, their anger, she could only imagine. *Oh, what have I done?*

The body was still prone on the top step of the veranda. Her shot had struck Danny square in the chest. Death had been almost instantaneous.

"You did exactly what you were supposed to do." Springer had crouched beside her. He was talking like a coach preparing her for the last game of the season. "You followed procedure every step of the way. Don't worry, Kelly. You're young…you'll get over this. Everything's going to work out fine."

The arrival of the team from Calgary had transformed the quiet crime scene into a bustling center of activity. Kelly watched the photographer check the lighting before taking some stills of the body. Someone else leaned over to examine the bullet wound in the victim's chest.

So much blood.

Kelly looked away. A woman approached her from one of the parked police cars. Mid-thirties, short dark hair, tentative smile. Probably with Member Assistance. Springer obviously thought so, too. He let go of Kelly's shoulder and stood.

"Staff Sergeant Springer," he said, stepping forward to meet the new arrival.

"Corporal Webster," said the woman.

Kelly glanced back at the body. One of the Ident men was making a chalk outline of the victim's position on the rotting wood porch. From the corner of her eye, Kelly noticed movement from the back of the house.

The victim's brother, Mick Mizzoni, also the editor of the *Canmore Leader,* was coming to check things out. He'd been en route to Calgary when Dylan had called him on Sharon's instructions. As a result, he'd made it here even before the squad cars from Canmore. Now the broodily handsome man circled the busy police officers, his body visibly tense, his expression grim.

Abruptly he switched directions to face her. Kelly didn't allow herself to shift her gaze or even blink. She felt his condemnation, the current of loathing traveling from man to woman the way electrical energy had passed from clouds to earth in the storm earlier.

As the moment between them stretched, she fought back the instinct to tell him she was sorry. No matter what words she chose, they would come out sounding trite.

Besides, apologies for homicides were rarely accepted.

CHAPTER ONE

Two months later

"I WENT TO SEE the kids again today." Kelly Shannon slouched into the tartan cushions of Scott Martin's sofa.

"Kelly...was that wise?" At the other end of the couch, Scott propped his feet on the maple table, where he kept a dish of white peppermints and coasters for the coffee, water or tea he offered at the beginning of each session.

Kelly always took water. Now she swirled it in her glass, but the ice cube lodged at the bottom wouldn't move. It was too big, or else the glass was too small.

"I know what you said about moving on. But I just can't do it." One of the worst consequences of being suspended was all the free time. She'd signed up for some volunteer assignments with a local charity, but had found it difficult to concentrate on all but the simplest of tasks.

"Kelly, spying on those kids is only making matters worse—"

"I *know.*" They circled the same issues at each weekly session. If she didn't like Scott as much as she did, the sessions would be unbearable.

But Scott was okay. Over the past two months they'd achieved a certain comfort level in their weekly chats. Word had it he was happily married and totally besotted by his twin four-year-old daughters. You'd never know by his office, though. He didn't have any framed pictures of his family on display. When she'd asked him about it once, his answer had surprised her.

"Lots of the clients I see are working through problems at home, with their marriage or their kids. They don't need me throwing my domestic bliss in their face."

It was that kind of sensitivity that made her respect Scott Martin—even though, in her heart, she knew these compulsory sessions weren't doing the slightest bit of good. But her sisters had insisted, and Kelly figured it wasn't worth arguing over.

"I'm not sure if I'll ever want to go back to work, anyway," she said. Definitely not in any capacity where she'd have to carry a gun.

"You say that now, Kelly, but it's only been two months."

Two months, where each day was worse than the one before it....

"Do you know what they were wearing, Scott? Pajamas! In November. And it was snowing." Kelly leaned forward, cupping her hands over her knees. She could picture them so clearly, playing in the soft powder of a fresh snowfall, their little faces as solemn as if they were sitting in the front pew at church.

Every now and then the eldest, Billy, who was just five, had glanced in the direction of her car. Did he know who she was, what she'd done?

"And I don't think their mother is feeding them properly. Even though I leave groceries by the door every week." She'd never seen Sharon throw them away, but there were never any cooking odors coming from the small bungalow on First Avenue, either.

"Have you phoned Child Welfare?"

Annoyance propelled her to her feet. "Don't piss me off, Scott." She prowled the office, as she did every week, checking his bookcase for new volumes, examining the clean sweep of his polished maple desk, peering out the double-paned glass window at the Calgary traffic on Memorial Drive. Beyond the twin ribbons of concrete stood a row of mature, albeit heavily pruned, cottonwoods, planted to commemorate the veterans of the First World War. Beyond those, the Bow River. Follow that river upstream about an hour—and there would be Canmore. The mountain town she'd lived in all her life.

After training, she'd been stationed in northern

Saskatchewan for about six years, but she'd petitioned hard to be returned to the place of her birth. Her middle sister, Cathleen, still lived there, although their elder sister Maureen had a legal practice here in Calgary.

"You've been put in a difficult situation, Kelly. Society generally accepts that while killing is wrong, it may be necessary in some situations to preserve order and protect the lives of the innocent. Intellectually, most of us accept that."

Kelly stared out the window and nodded.

"This places a terrible onus of responsibility on the police officer entrusted to make these life-and-death decisions."

Kelly said nothing. She and Scott had tromped over the moral and ethical issues so many times, the field was flattened. She supposed he thought that if he repeated himself often enough, she'd find absolution. The very idea was ridiculous.

"Kelly, you will learn to cope with this. I promise."

Scott's voice betrayed the pain he felt for her. That was something else she liked about him. The man cared.

Unfortunately, in her case, it couldn't help.

Because she'd killed a man. And even if society decided she'd been acting within the rules by doing so, there was no way to avoid her moral culpability. The only remaining question was, how could she atone for taking another human life? If it was even possible.

KELLY HAD EVERY INTENTION of returning to her basement apartment after her late-afternoon session with Scott, but once she was back within Canmore's town limits, the right-hand turn onto Bow Valley Trail compelled her. Soon she cruised past the tiny bungalow that Sharon Mizzoni rented. She parked her truck on the opposite side of the street, down the block a few houses. Turning her key onto auxiliary power so she wouldn't waste gas, she continued to listen to a talk show on the CBC.

An hour passed. Maybe two. Outside it was dark and light now glowed from the small front window of the house, blending with the blue glare of the television set. The drapes weren't drawn, and Kelly could see directly into the living room. Sharon sat in front of the set, a beer bottle in her hand. Three-year-old Amanda jumped on the sofa. There was no sign of Billy.

Kelly didn't think the kids had been fed any dinner. It was almost eight. They should be having baths and brushing their teeth, getting ready for bed. Why wasn't Sharon helping them?

With the heat off, the truck was cool. Frosty wind from the Rocky Mountains was forecast to bring more snow to Canmore this evening. Kelly zipped the down vest she wore over her fleece jacket, then slipped on leather gloves. She'd stay until the cold forced her on, or until the lights went out.

But the lights generally went out late at Sharon Mizzoni's house. The death of her husband, Danny, had hit her hard and she'd turned to alcohol for solace. At times, Kelly almost envied her. She, too, longed for chemically induced oblivion. Drugs, alcohol, even an overdose of sleeping pills. Kelly had considered all of them in the darkest hours of these past months.

But two things stood in her way. Her sisters. And Sharon's kids.

Kelly had always been in awe of her older sisters—Cathleen with her confident beauty and effortless appeal to members of the opposite sex, Maureen with her brains and her take-charge attitude. The two of them would never hold with her choosing the chicken's way out—ending her own life. Probably, they'd haul her up from the grave and tell her Christmas dinner was going to be at her place for the next twenty years.

In the Mizzoni house, Billy had just come into view from the window. Kelly observed him pick up his little sister and carry her off down the hall. Probably taking the three-year-old to bed. Kelly had seen the same routine on previous nights, and, as always, her heart ached for the kids.

She wanted nothing more than to go into that house and mother those children. But she knew if she got out of her car, she'd end up in trouble. Sharon had noticed her hanging around before, and warned her to stay far, far away.

But that was impossible.

Kelly rubbed at the condensation forming on the inside of her truck's window. On the radio Shania Twain was feeling like a woman. Stuck here in her four-by-four, Kelly felt hardly human.

If she hadn't shot Danny Mizzoni, those kids would still have a father, and Sharon wouldn't be drinking. Like a roller coaster forced to travel the same circuit again and again, she lived through those short seconds that had forever changed so many lives. Danny bringing out his gun, pointing it at her sister Cathleen...

Her shouted warning. "Police. Drop the gun, Danny!"

Danny's stupid, knee-jerk reaction—cocking his weapon, bringing it up to Cathleen's head....

Kelly had been trained to preserve life. She'd also been trained to make difficult choices. When Cathleen fell away from Mizzoni's grasp, leaving him exposed, Kelly didn't have to think. Her training took over. She aimed for the center of his body, as was RCMP policy.

BAM! The shot left her gun before she fully comprehended what she was doing. Instantly dead, Danny had loosened his hold on his gun. His blood had splattered on the rotting porch boards.

God, God, God... Kelly reached to turn up the volume on the radio. At that moment, a knock at her side window sent her heart slamming against her chest. She turned to see a man's torso, his bare hand still rapping on the glass by her head.

Her panic subsided. Quite certain who this was, she unrolled her window with trembling fingers.

The man stooped, and she saw his face. His handsome, almost beautiful face, framed with thick dark hair. "On surveillance, Officer?"

The bitter question came from the children's uncle, Mick Mizzoni. Before the shooting she and he had had an amicable relationship. He'd often come to her for police information when he was working on a story for the *Canmore Leader*. They'd crossed paths now and then in social settings, too—at the wedding of a mutual friend; a couple of times at the Canmore Folk Festival.

She'd half entertained a hope he might ask her out. But behind Mick's casual banter had always been an almost imperceptible coolness. She'd assumed she simply wasn't his type.

And that was before she'd killed his brother.

"Mick." Kelly couldn't meet his quiet, intense gaze for long. She glanced back at the house, not able to find the words to remind him she was on temporary leave from the RCMP. Undoubtedly he knew, and was only baiting her, anyway.

Mick Mizzoni had to hate her, and Kelly didn't blame him. Mostly she hated herself, too.

"The children should be in bed," she said.

Mick frowned, the expression not diminishing his attractiveness one iota. He wore a denim jacket over a rough wool sweater. Warm, substantial clothing that emphasized his masculinity.

"How the hell do you know?"

"I can see them through the window. Billy just carried Amanda to the bedroom. Sharon's been drinking—" she glanced at the digital clock on her dash "—for at least two hours."

Mick yanked open the door that separated them. "How long have you been sitting here?"

When she got out of the truck, she noticed that Mick backed off several steps. As if he couldn't stand to be too close.

"Does it matter? What's important is the kids. I don't think they've even had supper. Most nights Sharon doesn't move from the television."

He cursed. "I know she's drinking again. God, I'd hoped she'd finally put that life behind her..."

But her husband's death had been too much for her to handle. "What can we do to help them?"

"We?" Mick's voice had been relatively calm. Now she saw him struggle to regain that equilibrium.

"Kelly, I'm trying my damnedest not to blame you for what happened. I know Danny had a gun on your sister. I know you were trying to do your job. But given the consequences of that, maybe you ought to stay the hell away from Danny's family.''

''I'm sorry.'' She understood what he was saying, totally accepted that they all had to hate her for what she'd done. But it was because of her responsibility for Danny's death that she couldn't walk away from his kids. If she tried to explain, would Mick understand?

''Get in your truck, Kelly, and drive back to the right side of town.''

''But—''

He opened the truck door wider. She ignored him. The lights from Sharon's window were irresistible. She advanced along the snow-packed road, until she stood in front of the small bungalow.

A moment later, Mick joined her. Together they watched Sharon tip the bottle of beer up to her mouth and suck back the last drop.

''The kids are *my* responsibility. I'm their uncle. Please leave, Kelly.''

''I can't.'' She swallowed the need to weep. Her tears would lead this man to not only hate her, but despise her, as well. Besides, what right did she have to give in to her pain, when he had to be suffering just as much?

Mick shifted his weight impatiently. ''You aren't helping anything by putting in time here. In fact, you could be making the situation worse. If Sharon notices you, she could freak out—''

''I know.'' Sharon had seen her leaving behind a bag of groceries once, and she'd come out the back door screaming and yelling. But she'd taken the food inside, and so Kelly hadn't stopped. She'd just tried to be quieter the next time.

''For good reason.''

''I realize that, Mick. But she's not capable of being a mother to those kids right now.''

''I'm doing my best to help.''

She knew that, too. She'd seen him coming and going, often carrying a bag from a takeout restaurant. This was the first time, though, that he'd approached her before going inside.

''Whatever you're able to do, it's not enough. They were playing in the snow with only their pajamas on this morning. And Billy's looking awfully pale. I think he's lost weight—''

Mick slammed a hand against the trunk of a nearby tree. A dusting of snow was released into the air, and Kelly watched the flakes settle against the dark blue of his jacket.

''She loves those kids,'' he said.

''I'm sure she must.''

''And they love *her*. You have no idea how devoted Billy is to his mother. You can't think we should try to get them taken away from her?''

Had he noticed he'd used the word *we?* Kelly

doubted it. "Mick, because of me they lost their father. I don't want them to lose their mother, too."

Mick considered that statement for a moment, before nodding. "Good. 'Cause no way is Child Welfare getting involved in this case. If Danny's family needs help, then I'm the one to give it to them."

"No question those kids need you, Mick. You're their uncle. But what I wonder is…" She hesitated. Who was she to point fingers?

"Yeah?"

Deciding the welfare of the children called for honesty, she continued. "Well, with the hours you put in at the paper, and the way Sharon's been drinking…something really bad could happen to them, Mick. They need more."

They need me. Kelly didn't voice the last part, but the conviction that she had to help this family remained.

CHAPTER TWO

AFTER MICK HAD GONE INSIDE to check on Billy and Amanda, Kelly returned to her truck. Instead of heading to her basement apartment on the other side of town, she cruised back to the highway, almost instinctively drawn to the Larch Lodge Bed and Breakfast, which Cathleen had renovated several years ago.

Cathleen and Dylan wouldn't be there. They'd flown to Vegas for a delayed honeymoon, leaving Poppy O'Leary to run the place for the week. Seventy-year-old Poppy had been staying there for about six months now, working on her family tree and a treasury of favorite recipes. During the weeks after the shooting, when Kelly had been a guest at the B and B, too, she and Poppy had become quite close.

Kelly eased off the accelerator and coasted the final yards of the laneway. Now in full view of the house, she could see Poppy's mop of artificial-red curls as she worked at the kitchen sink in front of the window. Probably she was organizing tomorrow's breakfast for the guests. Three unknown vehicles were parked, along with Poppy's red Tracker, at the side of the house. Kelly left her truck at the end of the line, then headed for the side veranda.

"Poppy?" Kelly stuck her head inside the door. Cathleen's dog looked at her lazily, managing only a slight wag of his tail. Curled up beside him was a beautiful white cat, the latest addition to Cathleen's menagerie. Dylan had adopted Crystal shortly after his mother's death, and Crystal had promptly adopted Kip as her closest buddy. A relationship Kip tolerated but obviously did not enjoy.

"Kelly! I was hoping you'd show up. Come on in and sit. I've got a new muffin recipe for you to sample."

Poppy's solution to every problem was food. Which was ironic given that the common Shannon family reaction to stress was an aversion to eating. Kelly knew she'd dropped pounds since the shooting, and Cathleen was just now regaining the weight she'd lost during the two years she and Dylan had been estranged. Then there was Maureen, who'd looked not only too slender at her last visit, but too pale, as well. Of course, only six months had passed since her husband's death.

"You must think we Shannons are a sorry bunch." Kelly tore the paper liner off the still-warm muffin. She could see sunflower seeds and raisins peeking out from the golden-brown crust. The aroma of honeyed spices was enticing.

"Every family has its hard times." Poppy took a glass measure and poured in milk. She popped the milk into the microwave to heat, then mixed a paste of cocoa and sugar in Kelly's favorite ceramic mug.

Bless her heart, she was making the hot chocolate that Kelly loved.

"I was looking at the cottonwoods on Memorial Drive today, and thinking." She could see the dark trunks in her mind's eye, the bare winter branches reaching, almost desperately, to the sky.

"When you were in Calgary?"

Poppy knew about her weekly sessions with the RCMP counselor.

"Yes. I really feel for those war vets coming home and having to deal with the atrocities they'd seen and participated in overseas."

"Times were different then. The men knew they'd done their duty for their country. On their return, they were treated like heroes."

"Do you really think it was that simple, Poppy?"

The microwave beeped, and Poppy took out the steaming milk. "No," she admitted, "I guess not."

"Compared with what they went through, my experience is pure Little League."

Poppy set the mug of hot chocolate in front of her. "It doesn't *feel* Little League, though, does it?"

Kelly pressed her lips tightly together and shook her head. With both hands she cupped the warm mug. In the end, despite the appetizing aroma, she'd been unable to stomach the muffin. This she could handle. She took a sip, and the creamy, warm liquid glided down her throat.

"You take everything so much to heart." Poppy's old eyes contained warmth and compassion—benefactions Kelly knew she didn't deserve, but craved so desperately.

Poppy laid a hand on her arm. "You're such a softy, aren't you, love. And your sisters have no idea. They see you as strong and stalwart."

"I *am* strong. I'm the youngest, but I've always looked out for Cath and Maureen. They tease me about being a mother hen...."

"Those two! They're so impulsive and confident. They don't know how it feels to be otherwise. I'm sure they've never even guessed how badly your father's desertion hurt you."

"Oh!" It was unbelievable how Poppy always honed in on the important things. Kelly had spoken of those feelings to no one. Not even to her mother when she'd been alive. Now Kelly regarded this amazing woman with a touch of awe.

"How can you understand us so well, when you've only known us such a short time?"

Poppy's hand tightened on Kelly's forearm. "My dear Kelly, it isn't hard. You were a sensitive child, living in a house full of self-assured, outgoing women. It's not that they didn't love you to death. From all I've heard about your mother, I know she did, and your sisters still do. They just aren't equipped to understand...."

Tears again were too close. Kelly sipped more liquid, then found herself wanting to tell Poppy more. "I was just a baby when Dad left. I didn't even know him. How could I miss him?"

Poppy leaned back in her chair. She was quiet, but Kelly didn't mind the silence. Her head was too full of her own thoughts.

She knew the story of her father's restlessness, recounted endlessly by her elder sisters when they were kids. After each baby was born, he'd left their mother for a while, always to return about a year later.

Except the last time.

"What was wrong with me, Poppy? How come he didn't come back for me, like he did for the others?"

"Oh, love. He missed so much, your dad."

But what he'd missed had been by his choice. That was what was so hard for Kelly to accept. As a kid she'd made up stories to take that choice away. He'd been in an accident and suffered from amnesia.... He'd been arrested for a crime he hadn't committed and didn't want them to know he'd been sent to jail....

Of course, as an adult, and a cop, she could no longer delude herself. She knew the statistics on how many men walked away from their families, never to be heard from again. These things just had to be accepted.

"Poppy, I had a happy childhood. And even though we didn't have a father and money was kind of tight, we were much better off than so many children I see in my line of work."

Which brought her thoughts back to Billy and Amanda. And to their uncle, whose sad face had been haunting under the glow of the streetlight. His intentions were good, but what could he really do to help the situation?

What could any of them do? Kelly swallowed the last of her cocoa. She wished she could curl up here all night, warm and cozy in Poppy's kitchen.

"Would you like to stay over, love?" Poppy asked, reading her mind yet again. "The rooms are full, but there's the pullout couch in the study."

"Thanks, Poppy, but I'd better get home." When she woke in the night, as she always did, it was better not to have to worry about waking anyone else. Besides, once Poppy left the room, the magic of this place was gone.

"I guess it's time I was leaving."

"You didn't eat your muffin. Shall I wrap a few for your breakfast?"

Kelly didn't have the heart to say no.

SHARON WAS TOTALLY WASTED. At least a half-dozen empty bottles of beer were strewn on the floor. Mick could hear her snoring on the sofa as he stepped out of the children's room. He was thankful they'd finally fallen asleep. Amanda had dropped off quickly, but poor Billy had been full of his usual questions.

Where was his dad, and how long would he be dead? The kid just couldn't seem to grasp the concept of *forever*. Which was maybe a blessing.

Mick stepped over some scattered building blocks on his way to the bathroom. The sink was a mess. He cleaned it, then grabbed the laundry basket Sharon kept next to the tub. Full again.

This house didn't come with a washer or drier, and Sharon wasn't often capable of making it to the Laundromat, so he'd started doing the family's laundry at home. If he left now, he'd get a load done before bed, but he hated to go with Sharon passed out like that.

What if there was a problem with one of the kids during the night? Sharon might not hear them.

He returned to the kitchen, where a box of sugar-coated cereal and two dirty glasses gave him a good idea of what the kids had eaten for dinner. He picked up one of the plastic tumblers and sniffed.

Cola.

Opening the fridge, he saw a carton of milk, unopened. The liter of cola, however, was almost all gone.

Well, he couldn't blame the kids. If he were five, he supposed he'd make the same menu choices.

But what was Sharon eating? As far as he could tell, these days her diet was purely liquid.

Halfway through cleaning up the kitchen, Mick collapsed onto one of the chairs.

What the hell was he going to do?

From the living room came a protracted groan. Good, Sharon was waking. He put on a pot of coffee and popped two slices of whole wheat bread into the toaster.

"Oh, God…what time is it?" Sharon's voice held a touch of panic.

He went to check on her. "Almost ten. How do you feel?"

Sharon could be a pretty girl when she made an effort, but booze and a general disregard for cleanliness did not bring out her best attributes. Mick felt like throwing her in the shower. Instead, he held out a hand and pulled her into the kitchen.

"Did the kids have dinner?" Sharon asked, sinking into a kitchen chair.

"Dry cereal and cola."

"Good."

Mick caught the ghostly flash of her sardonic smile.

"This isn't working out, you know," he said. He put a mug of black coffee in front of her. "Drink this. Then eat some toast."

She pushed the plate away. "I can't. Just the smell makes me nauseous."

"Too bad. Your body needs food." He slid the plate back to her, watching as with shaking hands she lifted the mug to her mouth.

"You must be getting sick of baby-sitting us, Mick."

"I'll do what I've got to do. But you have to start feeding those kids right, and getting them to bed at a decent hour." He thought about Kelly Shannon's comment about their pajamas. "And put them in their snowsuits when they go outside to play."

"I know, I know." Sharon closed her eyes and rubbed at her forehead.

"I'm serious. They're going to get sick."

"I'm trying, Mickey. I'm doing the best I can."

He believed her. The best she could do was worthless, though, as long as she was drinking. "You need to get back on the program, Sharon. The way you did before Amanda was born."

When he'd found out his brother and his wife were expecting their second child, he'd all but dragged them to that first meeting, worried about what Sharon's drinking could do to her unborn child. It was still a miracle to him that Billy had turned out so normal.

His suggestion had Sharon crying now. "I can't go, Mickey. I can't stop drinking with Danny gone. It's too soon. I'm not ready."

"Sure it's hard, but you've got to be strong. You've got to think of your kids."

The tears came faster; Sharon's sobs hiccuped, then intensified.

"I can't do this. I'm so alone...."

He reached over to stroke her head. "I'm here, Sharon. I'll help you."

"I don't see how you can."

"I'll take you to the meetings, help you with the kids."

Sharon shook her head. "And what about the new one?"

"Huh?"

"I'm pregnant, Mickey. The new baby will be here in seven months."

MICK DIDN'T DRINK. There was too much alcoholism in his family. His mother *and* his brother. Probably his father, too, although unlike his half brother, Danny, he'd never figured out exactly who that was.

So Mick did what he always did when he couldn't sleep. Sat in his darkened living room and stared out the large picture window. A nearby streetlamp cast a dull yellow light on the road and the houses beyond, but it didn't really matter, because Mick wasn't paying any attention to the view. The problems of his brother's family were too heavy in his mind.

What the hell was he going to do about Amanda

and Billy? Kelly was right; the situation was poised for disaster. With his years of journalism, it was all too easy to imagine his family in the headlines again.

Two Children Killed In House Fire. Mother too drunk to call 911....

Children Hospitalized For Malnutrition. Mother currently under police investigation....

If only Danny hadn't died. The family had finally been doing okay. Sharon hadn't fallen off the wagon once since Amanda's birth. Danny's job with Max Strongman had lasted over a year—his longest period of steady employment ever.

Then Mick thought of the stash of illegal drugs the police had found in one of the barns when they'd searched the Thunder Bar M after Danny's death, and knew he was fooling himself. Danny hadn't been as rehabilitated as he'd hoped.

The red light on his answering machine caught his eye, but he just turned away. If it was work, they'd try his cell. As for his friends, well, he no longer had time for the mountain biking and cross-country skiing that had formerly occupied his nonworking hours. He'd given up all his leisure activities to look after Danny's kids.

And Kelly was right again. It wasn't enough. Especially now that there was a third child on the way. To think of how much drinking Sharon had been doing these past two months made Mick sick. She'd promised she would shower in the morning and get ready for him to take her to the doctor. Later in the week, he'd try to convince her to go back to AA.

But that was all he could do for her. And in his heart he knew it wasn't enough.

So what were his options?

Mick stretched out his legs and leaned his head back. The most obvious solution was one he could hardly bring himself to think about, let alone seriously consider.

He could marry Sharon and take responsibility for his brother's family.

Every cell in his body, though, protested that route. That he didn't love Sharon, had never even liked her, wasn't the main problem. He didn't see how he could partner up with a woman he couldn't respect. His mother had been a drunk. He couldn't, just couldn't, marry another one. Especially one who put the bottle ahead of her children.

But if he didn't marry Sharon, where did that leave him?

As Kelly had said—God, every point the woman had made had been bang on—he didn't have the time to look after them himself. He supposed he could seek custody, then hire a nanny.

But those kids needed permanence—a family, a home. He loved them as if they were his own. Wanted them to have everything he and his brother had never had.

A mom *and a dad*. Regular bedtimes and meal-times. Clean clothes, and a cake and a few gifts on their birthdays....

The more he thought about it, the more Mick came to realize that his first instincts had been right. Marriage was the solution. Just not to Sharon.

CHAPTER THREE

"HEY, KIDS! Here's a new cereal you'll really like. It's got marshmallows and chocolate and..."

Billy Mizzoni's stomach growled. He turned away from the cheerful TV commercial and looked at his sister on the couch beside him. "Hungry, Mandy?"

His sister nodded. She had her thumb in her mouth and was holding the flannel blanket that was supposed to be for her doll.

It was weird. His sister hadn't sucked her thumb when she was a baby, but now she did. She'd also stopped talking, and had started peeing her pants at night.

He didn't mind the stopped-talking part, but the accidents at night were getting to him, since they shared the same bed.

"Come on." Billy led the way to the kitchen. It was all tidy again, like it usually was after Uncle Mick came to visit. He opened the bottom cupboard and surveyed boxes of cereal and crackers. Most he didn't recognize. That made him suspicious. They might have vegetables or something in them. He reached for the golden box that had once been his favorite, the type they'd just seen advertised on TV.

Amanda made a face when he poured some into a bowl for her. Maybe she was getting sick of it, just like he was. But he didn't know what else to give her.

In the old days, before his daddy went to heaven, his mom usually made them toast and gave them juice in the mornings. But she was still sleeping now. He kind of hoped she'd keep sleeping a long time. She'd been sick a lot since Daddy died.

Billy went to the fridge but couldn't find the left-over pop from last night. A carton of milk had been pushed into its place, and it even had the spout opened.

Oh, well. He picked it up and poured some into each of their bowls. Mandy looked surprised. They usually ate their cereal dry.

"There isn't any pop," he explained.

She shrugged and picked up her spoon.

Billy gobbled down his cereal in a flash. Boy, he was really hungry. But the cereal didn't taste as yummy as usual. He'd almost prefer toast and peanut butter, the way Mommy used to make it.

He supposed she'd make it again, once Daddy got back from this "forever" place that Uncle Mick kept talking about. Hopefully soon. Billy missed him, although he didn't miss the lickings that were supposed to make him "grow up right."

"Want to play outside?" he asked his sister.

Again, Mandy just nodded. No matter what he asked her, she always agreed.

"We could make a fort. It snowed again last night." He thought that might get her excited, but she just moved her head up and down and waited calmly for him to lead the way.

At the side door, Billy saw boots and mittens propped right in his path. Next to them lay the snowsuits Uncle Mick had bought them a few weeks ago. They were complicated things with legs attached to the coat part. It was easier to put on lighter jackets and runners. It wasn't *that* cold outside.

Unlatching the screen, he had to shield his eyes from the sun. Gosh, the snow was deep. They'd be able to make a great fort. He grabbed Mandy's little hand and half dragged her to the front yard. Once there, he glanced automatically to the street. Would that lady be sitting in her car watching them again?

Sure enough, there she was. Just about every day since his dad had died, he'd seen her. Watching him and Mandy, as if she was an angel or something, sent by his dad. He'd seen a movie like that, once on TV.

He wondered if she had any magical powers. But so far he hadn't seen signs of any.

ALMOST TWO WEEKS LATER, Mick had made important strides in finding himself a wife. He shut down his computer for the night and was grabbing his coat from the rack by the window, when the door to his office swung open. Expecting that Abby had decided to meet him here, rather than at the restaurant, he turned with a smile.

Which quickly disappeared when the mayor of Canmore, Max Strongman, entered the room. Tall and still handsome in his fifties, the mayor appeared to feel he had every right to be showing up well past office hours.

"Taking off, were you?" Max made it sound as though it were slothful for Mick to be leaving the office at seven in the evening. With all the assurance of someone used to calling the shots, he settled into the chair opposite Mick's desk.

Reluctantly, Mick returned to his own seat. "I've got a date in ten minutes so I'm in a bit of a hurry." He glanced at his watch and thought of the reservation he'd made at Sinclair's, and Abby's proclivity to be on time.

"Don't worry. This isn't a social call. I'm worried about those grandchildren of mine. Word is, their mother's been doing a lot of drinking. Making a bit of a scene at the local bars."

That Max Strongman had been Danny's father was something Mick had only discovered after his brother's death. Somehow he'd never drawn the connection to Billy and Amanda, but of course Strongman was right. He was their grandfather.

"I'm worried, too," Mick confessed.

"Then, why don't you do something about it? I can't have my own grandkids turned into street urchins. Can you imagine how that would look to all my bleeding-heart voters?"

Mick had never liked Max Strongman, but in that instant, he hated him. The man didn't care about Billy's and Amanda's welfare. He was concerned about his public image.

A public image that Mick, in his weekly editorial, did his best to challenge whenever the facts would allow—which wasn't often, because Max was wily and smart and not prone to making mistakes.

For a time, Mick had wondered if he wasn't wrong about the mayor. But then Rose Strongman had been murdered, and his suspicions were renewed.

He had a soft spot for Strongman's deceased wife. Years ago, when she'd still been married to her first husband, she'd been at the elementary school as a volunteer helper and had noticed Mick languishing out in the school yard.

He could still remember how cool her palm had felt when she placed it to his forehead, and how sweet she'd smelled when she'd bent low to take his hand.

"You're sick, aren't you? What's your name, son?"

He'd told her, and immediately seen by her reaction that she'd connected him to his mother. He was used to people pulling away when they realized who he really was.

But Rose McLean—as she was then—had asked the principal for permission to take him home. She put him in her own son's bed, served him broth and gave him medicine. Never in his life had he received so much attention.

Then she'd phoned his mother and asked for permission to keep him overnight. She'd said he was good company for her own son, Dylan, although in truth the older boy had barely deigned to notice him. The next day, unfortunately, his fever had broken, and after lunch she'd driven him back to school. He'd had a bath and was wearing a new pair of jeans and a sweatshirt. His mother never asked him about the clothes, and he'd never forgotten Rose Strongman's wonderful act of charity.

So watching the changes in her character during her long marriage to Strongman had torn at his gut. Several times over the years he'd gone to her, offering to help if she'd let him. Every time she'd pretended that she was ill, that Max was a caring husband, that he shouldn't worry.

And then suddenly it was too late. She was dead, murdered in her own living room. After weeks of investigation—focused primarily on her son, Dylan—the evidence had begun to point to Max Strongman's son, James. Before the police could question him, James disappeared following a one-way flight to Puerto Vallarta, Mexico. Not only was Mick convinced that Max was behind his son's disappearance, he also suspected he may have had a hand in the crime itself.

Of course, he dared not print a word of his suspicions in the paper without evidence. Evidence that probably didn't exist.

Now Mick glared at the man in front of him, and wished he had the nerve to tell him to go to hell. But Max's biological ties to the children made him nervous. "What, exactly, do you expect me to do?"

Strongman seemed to take a perverse pleasure in Mick's hostility. He smiled, satisfied and confident, as he leaned back in his chair. "I expect you to take custody of those kids and see to it they're raised right."

"What about their mother?"

"She's trash. Forget about her."

Mick doubted it would be that easy for Billy and Amanda. "The situation's a bit more complicated, don't you think?"

"Tell you what." Strongman leaned over his legs, shortening the distance between their faces. "Either you take control of those kids or I will."

Mick went silent in his shock. Was Strongman serious? Would he apply to the courts for custody of his grandchildren? One thing Mick knew for sure—he couldn't stand to see Billy and Amanda raised by this man.

"I'll see what I can do," he said.

"Good." Strongman got to his feet and dusted off his pants as if he'd been sitting in something soiled. "I expect you to live up to that, or you'll be hearing from me."

"WOULD YOU LIKE DESSERT, ABBY?"

Mick glanced at his watch as he took a sip of water. Nine-thirty. He hoped the kids were in bed and that Sharon was sticking to her promise not to drink. He'd taken her to an AA meeting yesterday, after her doctor's appointment, but she'd attended reluctantly and that wasn't a good sign.

"I'm not sure." His date surveyed the choices on the menu. "Are you in a hurry?" Her gaze shifted to his watch, and he realized she'd noticed him checking the time.

"No. Absolutely not. I was thinking I might like the mixed berry crisp."

Abby smiled. "Sounds good."

Mick held in a sigh and signaled the waiter. "Two crisps, please. And a coffee for me."

"And you, miss?" the waiter asked. "More wine, perhaps?"

"Oh, no. I'll have coffee, too. Only make mine decaf."

Mentally, Mick ticked off a point in her favor.

This was their fifth date and so far he hadn't seen her drink more than one glass of wine in an evening.

Really, on all counts she was perfect. He credited his screening process for that. He'd asked her out because she was a kindergarten teacher. That had to mean she liked small kids, he'd figured. And sure enough, every time she discussed her work, her face took on a warm glow. He'd noticed she also had a soft spot for animals. They couldn't pass a dog on the street without her stopping.

As far as Mick was concerned, he was ready to propose right this minute. The visit from Max Strongman had increased the pressure on his need to marry—and quickly. If it came to a custody show-down between him and Strongman, surely the fact that he had a wife and could offer a two-parent home would stand in his favor.

But although he sensed Abby liked him a lot, he did think she'd consider that moving a bit *too* quickly.

"Are you worried about something, Mick?"

Her hand felt warm and gentle on his arm, re-minding him of the one minor problem with this courtship. He wasn't really attracted to her, had never felt the urge to go beyond their tender but brief good-night kisses.

That would change with time, he was sure. Abby was cute and blond, with generous curves in all the right places.

"A little, I guess." He smiled and took her hand in his. "I'm sorry I'm not being very good company."

He watched as rosy color filled her cheeks. "That's okay. I just hope I haven't been boring you with my stories."

"Not at all," he said, meaning it. More than anything, he enjoyed her vignettes about the children in her class. It was so obvious how much she cared for all of them.

"It's just that some of my past boyfriends haven't been that interested. But I guess you must like kids."

"I do." *Two in particular.*

Abby must have read his mind. "How old are your niece and nephew?"

"Amanda's the baby. She's only three. Billy just turned five."

"Does he go to kindergarten?"

Mick frowned. "Not that I know of."

Abby shook her head. "He should have registered this fall. I suppose his father's death..."

Mick wondered if that was why Sharon hadn't enrolled him. But Danny had died mid-September, several weeks into the school year.

"I'll look into it, Abby. Is it too late for him to start this year?"

"No, of course not."

"Good." As coffee and dessert were delivered,

Mick took stock of the evening. It might be too early to ask Abby to be his wife, but maybe the time was right for her to meet the kids.

"How would you feel about going out for pizza on Friday?" he asked.

"Really?" She sounded surprised.

"Yeah. I thought I might bring Billy and Amanda along. Give Sharon a bit of a break."

"Well, that's a nice idea, but, Mick, I'm not really sure if we should continue to see each other."

Whoa! Mick froze. Had he been reading the signals wrong, then? He'd been so sure she was interested in him. "Don't like pizza?" he said, trying to sound lighthearted.

Abby's smile appeared sad. "Don't get me wrong, Mick. I've enjoyed going out with you. But the feeling isn't mutual, is it?"

"I *like* you, Abby. Very much, in fact."

"You don't kiss me as if you like me," she said frankly. "And you don't... Oh, I don't know. It's hard to put into words."

"I realize I'm kind of reserved. People are always telling me that."

Her eyes brightened a little.

"Give us a bit more time, Abby. To get comfortable with each other."

"Are you sure that's what you want?"

"Absolutely." He squeezed her hand and hoped

that every warm feeling he had for her was reflected in his eyes.

The color in her face grew deeper. "Mick, if you had any idea..." Her voice trailed away, then she sighed. "Why don't you call me Thursday. We should *both* spend a few days thinking about where we're heading."

Straight to a justice of the peace. Of course, he couldn't say that. "Okay, Abby. If that's the way you want it."

She just sighed again, and he wondered what the hell had happened. They'd been off to such a promising start.

Maybe someone had filled her in on the Mizzoni family history, and that was where her doubts were springing from. Abby hadn't lived in Canmore all her life as he had. She'd moved here after graduation from the University of Calgary.

Perhaps she'd told one of her colleagues who she was dating, and they'd relayed the story about his mother, her drinking and her "boyfriends," then the trouble he and Danny had both courted in their youth. He'd straightened out in his teens, thanks to a wonderful man who'd volunteered for the Boy Scouts. Harvey Tomchuk had helped Mick see possibilities for a way of life Mick had always felt was out of reach.

An accountant in his day job, Harvey had soon discovered Mick's love of writing and convinced him to pursue a career in journalism. Now Mick was editor of the *Canmore Leader*, he owned a nice home, and he was, by most accounts, a respectable citizen.

But maybe Abby had heard some of the old stories and been turned off.

She didn't look turned off, though. Especially now as she caressed his wrist with her thumb. A gesture that was undoubtedly meant to be slightly erotic, but that he, instead, found slightly annoying.

"Mick?"

"Uh-huh?"

"What would you like to do now?"

Her voice invited him to think of activities in the bedroom. No way could he confess that what he really wanted was to drop her at home, then go to the house off Bow Valley Trail and check on the kids. He'd already come perilously close to blowing his chances with Abby.

"It's snowing outside. How about we take a walk, down to the river," he suggested.

"Oh, that sounds so romantic!"

Reprieve.

Mick signed the check for their meal with relief. Evidently, he'd finally said the right thing. Maybe this was going to work after all.

IT WAS ELEVEN by the time Mick made it to the little bungalow. Lights were still on, and he could hear loud music. What concerned him more was the string of vehicles parked on the street—including one newly familiar four-by-four truck.

Kelly Shannon spotted him before he reached the door to pound on her window again. She drew her long body out of the car—God, but she was thin. Her face appeared white and gaunt in the overhead glare from a streetlight.

For a long moment they stared at each other. His anger, justifiable though it was, sort of fizzled as he took in the dark smudges under her eyes and the grim, unhappy set of her mouth.

"What the hell is going on in there?" He turned toward the house. Through the front window, he could see almost a dozen people milling about in the small living room. The pounding of the bass from an overworked sound system marred the peaceful beauty of the winter night.

"The neighbors complained," Kelly said, "and the police were here about ten minutes ago. The party is finally breaking up."

As she spoke, the volume of the music dropped. A group of six appeared at the side door.

"'Night!" Sharon, barely able to stand, hung on to the iron railing on the landing as she saw her visitors out.

"Hey, baby."

"Keep in touch."

"My house next time."

A couple more guests spilled from the door. Few appeared as sloshed as Sharon did, which was fortunate, since they were getting into cars now. Mick watched, fighting rage.

How could she do this? It was as if she didn't care about the baby growing inside her. Or the two still-almost-babies who lived in that house with her.

He sensed Kelly slipping back into the shadow of a tree trunk. That was good. If Sharon saw her, she'd throw a fit. In her condition, the prospect was scary.

As the last car drove away, Sharon began to withdraw into the house. Mick took a few steps forward, catching her attention. Sharon held a hand to her forehead and scrunched up her eyes.

"Mick? That you?"

"Yeah, it's me. Where are the kids?"

"In bed. Sleeping."

With all that racket? He doubted it. "Let me see them."

Sharon shook her head. "Come back tomorrow. The party's over."

"I'm not interested in any bloody party. It's the kids I care about. Did you feed them any dinner, Sharon? Are they wearing clean pajamas?"

"Of course." Sharon spoke slowly, enunciating with the precision of someone who couldn't be sure just what would come out of her mouth.

"Let me see." He started for the door again, but she backed up, shaking her head.

"Tomorrow. My head hurts."

Of course your head hurts, you moron. He felt like shaking her. How much had she drunk tonight? He loped up the sidewalk, but by the time he reached the landing, Sharon had shut the door against him. The sound of the dead bolt closing was conspicuous in the now-quiet night.

Mick cursed and slammed his hand on the railing.

From behind him, he heard a rustling. Before he had time to turn, Kelly was speaking. "We've got to do something, Mick."

"I'm trying."

"I know." Her tone was placating. "But you haven't been over much lately."

Of course he hadn't. Because he was too damn busy courting the woman he wanted to take care of Amanda and Billy. The mother figure that Sharon appeared neither willing to be nor capable of being.

"I'm not blaming you, Mick."

"I would say not. If anyone was to be blamed..."

"I know—I know."

Kelly's quick acceptance of her culpability sapped the satisfaction out of lashing at her.

"If only Sharon could get a grip on herself. I took her to see a doctor and to an AA meeting." But she'd only gone because he'd made a fuss. He realized that she wouldn't make any progress in controlling her drinking unless it was something *she* wanted to do.

"To the doctor?"

"Sharon's pregnant."

Kelly gave a small gasp.

"Exactly." He dug his hands in the pockets of his denim jacket. "Just the complication Sharon needs right now, especially with—Kelly?"

The tall brunette put her hand to her mouth. Then she rushed to a hedge across the street. At the unmistakable sound of retching, Mick realized that Sharon's unborn baby added yet another layer to the former cop's guilt. He supposed he ought to have been more tactful.

He waited a minute, shuffling snow around with his feet. In his pocket, he had a paper napkin left over from lunch at the Bagel Bites Café. When Kelly was standing again, he went to her and offered it.

"Thanks." She turned away from him as she cleaned herself up.

"Don't take it so hard," he said, quelling an impulse to put a hand to her shoulder. "I've got a plan. I'm hoping to get married soon. Then I'm going to offer to take Sharon's children for a while, to give her a chance to settle down."

"Oh." Kelly's eyes were huge in her pale face. "Who are you marrying?"

"Well, I haven't asked her yet. But I'm hoping it'll be Abby Stevens."

"The kindergarten teacher?"

"Yeah. We've been dating for a while."

"Oh," she said again.

Somehow they both started walking along the road. The snow had stopped, but enough had fallen to turn the narrow street into a sparkling wonderland. Their boots crunched in the fresh drifts, and clouds of ice crystals formed with each exhaled breath.

"I know Abby," Kelly said at last. "She invites me to her class every fall to speak to the kids about Halloween safety." After a pause, she added, "She's cute."

"Yeah." He was beginning to think Abby was *too* cute, and that that was the problem. After their walk, he'd taken Abby home. At the door, he suspected, she had hoped for more than one short kiss good-night. But again, he'd felt no urge to carry things further.

"She'll be great with the kids," he said.

Kelly stopped walking, so he did, too. "You're in love with her, right?"

He bristled. "That's a little personal, don't you think?"

She took hold of his arm and forced him to face her. Those eyes of hers were so probing. And no wonder. She was a cop, after all.

"You're just marrying her because of the kids."

"Not real—" The denial jammed in his throat. That was the truth, so why not admit it? "Isn't that what marriage is all about? Raising kids. What does it matter if they aren't ours?''

"Of course it doesn't matter, Mick. But marriage is about more than kids.''

"Not in my book. Too many of the stories I cover for the paper are about tragedies that happen because parents don't put their children's interests first.'' Messy divorces, youngsters raised in poverty, family violence. God, he'd seen so many messed-up families. Not the least, his own brother's.

"Does Abby know how you feel about marriage? About her? She's always struck me as the romantic type.''

Mick freed the air trapped in his lungs. He didn't like the direction of Kelly's conversation. He had to marry Abby. If he didn't, he'd lose precious weeks of courting time; he didn't want to start from scratch with another woman.

"Why don't you hire a nanny instead of getting married?''

He'd thought about that option a lot. It had much to recommend it, but most of the benefits were to him, not the kids. "After all Billy and Mandy have been through, a nanny just isn't good enough.''

"I see.''

"Don't give me that look. If Abby agrees to marry me, I intend to be a good husband.''

"I'm sure that you do.''

Abruptly, Mick started back toward his vehicle.

Kelly stuck right beside him, her long stride easily matching his purposeful pace. At the door to his truck he paused to fish out his keys. The next thing he knew, Kelly had her hand over the lock.

"What are you doing?"

"Mick, I don't think you should marry Abby."

He swore for the second time that night. "And what about Billy and Amanda?" he asked. "I suppose you have a better idea how I can look after them?"

"As a matter of fact, I do," she said, her voice oddly calm.

"You can marry me."

CHAPTER FOUR

"YOU CAN'T BE SERIOUS." Mick concentrated on Kelly's determined expression. She didn't appear to be pulling his leg. Her suggestion that they marry was genuine.

A gust of wind flattened his hair and brought tears to his eyes. It was so cold out here, Kelly's lips had gone blue.

"Let's go to my place and talk," he suggested.

Kelly nodded. She hadn't spoken since telling him he should marry her. Perhaps she'd gone into shock. He opened his passenger door again and motioned her inside.

The drive to his house took less than five minutes—insufficient time for warm air to start blowing from the vehicle's heating system or even for the electric seat warmers to have much effect. He figured Kelly was even more frozen than he was by the time he had her sitting near the stoked-up fireplace in his living room. He left her holding her hands to the heat, while he put on coffee.

Coming back into the room, Mick took fresh stock of the woman. Tall and lean, she'd always given him the impression of athletic strength. Her brown hair was thick and shoulder length—he realized he was used to seeing it up in the bun she always wore when she was in uniform.

Up until the past two months, most of their encounters had occurred when they were both at work. When he needed information about RCMP activities, he'd always preferred asking Kelly. She had a quick, logical mind and a reserved nature that he felt comfortable with. He appreciated her sense of humor, too, which was subtle and slightly self-deprecating. Truthfully, he'd enjoyed her company so much, he'd been tempted to ask her out.

But given his past history in this town, he'd thought it safer to continue to date women outside the sphere of Canmore.

"Coffee will be ready in a few minutes. Are you getting warmer?"

"The feeling's back in my fingers," she said, still facing the fire. Her profile captivated him. He moved closer, to a chair just a few feet from where she was standing. From here, he could feel the heat from the fireplace, as well as continue to observe her.

"I understand that you must feel terrible about my brother." And he did. His journalistic training was too ingrained for him not to see both sides of the story. Despite his anger and grief at Danny's death, he knew that Kelly had only acted in accordance with RCMP procedure.

She'd shown up at the Thunder Bar M ranch in pursuit of her sister Cathleen and Dylan McLean. The intrepid couple, believing Danny had been involved in the murder of Dylan's mother, Rose, were determined to speak with him.

Ironically, it was Kelly's arrival on the scene that had panicked Danny—probably because of the stash of drugs he had hidden on the premises. Mick had read all the reports. He knew his brother had pulled a gun from his jacket and aimed it right at Cathleen.

He also knew that, by all accounts, Kelly had tried to defuse Danny's fear, speaking to him calmly and gently. But Danny had been too worked up. He'd cocked the trigger of his handgun, and that was it. Kelly had aimed, fired—

And Danny was dead.

Later, they'd discovered he'd played no part in Rose Strongman's death. And while the quantity of drugs he'd been storing would have seen him doing serious jail time, his life had been a high price to pay.

Still, Mick couldn't blame Kelly for his brother's foolish mistakes.

"Don't think it's guilt that's behind my suggestion," Kelly said now.

"What else could it be?" Mick wondered if she knew how much she'd changed since the shooting. Become thinner, quieter, more serious.

"Well, that's part of it," she admitted. "But it's way more complicated."

"I guess I can appreciate that."

"Mick, I genuinely care about those children. I would do anything to help them. Anything." She sat on the ottoman by his chair, leaning over her knees, entreating.

Something in him wanted to give her whatever she asked for. And, face it, she was offering him a solution to his own dilemma. But this was too important to decide impetuously.

"How will you feel in a year, or two, or ten? Kelly, I'm not interested in a temporary fix here."

"I understand that. I do."

In the small, bookshelf-lined room her words echoed like a marriage vow.

"Mick, you *have* to understand. I can't imagine what I'm going to do with my life if you say no. You know I'm suspended from police work. Once the attorney general's investigation into Danny's death is completed, I'll still have to wait out our own internal inquiry and the provincial fatality inquiry."

Mick was familiar with the process. Because of objectivity issues, he hadn't been covering the story in the *Leader,* but his number-one reporter was doing a thorough job. "How long will it take?"

"At best six months, assuming the attorney general doesn't lay criminal charges." Kelly ran her hands back over her head, pulling her hair tight from her face. "The thing is, even after all this is over, I can't imagine returning to police work."

Her eyes flooded and she bowed her head. Mick didn't know what to say. Kelly's pride in being a member of the Royal Canadian Mounted Police had always been evident. He could imagine his feelings if he had to abandon his journalism career.

"Maybe in time you'll feel differently."

She turned away from him. "You don't know how often I've heard those words—*in time*. Never from someone who's gone through what I have, who's *done* what I did. I killed a man. How could I go back to a job that required me to carry a gun?"

He didn't know. He also sensed this was hardly the time to suggest an administrative position of some kind. Kelly pleaded a strong case. But unwittingly she'd raised a major obstacle to her plan.

"Okay, Kelly. Say you leave the force forever when this is finally finished. How will Billy and Amanda feel about being raised by the woman who shot their father?"

Never mind *his* position. Marrying the police officer who'd killed his brother. God, he was crazy even to consider the idea.

"They're so young, Mick. Would they even understand what happened?"

How long is forever? "Not really," he admitted.

"Besides, we can't afford to worry about those

problems right now. I'm concerned their physical safety is at risk.''

And so was he. Sharon had probably passed out by now. He should've *insisted* on seeing the children, bundling them over to his house for the night. Friday he would. He'd take the afternoon off work, and tell Sharon she needed a break and he was looking after the kids for the weekend.

''Let me meet them, see how they react to being around me. Give me a chance, Mick.''

She wanted this so badly. And he couldn't take care of the children on his own. Could it be that this was the solution?

''Let's do it Friday,'' he said, thinking of the phone call he'd have to make to Abby. *You were right,* he'd tell her. *I haven't been fair to you.*

So was he being fair to Kelly? He didn't know. But at least he was being honest—they both were—about the reasons for contemplating a union.

''Do you like pizza?'' he asked.

''I love pizza. And Friday is perfect.''

''MICK MIZZONI is so gorgeous...''

The group of them were gathered in the study of the bed and breakfast. Dylan sat at the desk, recording deposits, while Cathleen, Poppy and Kelly ate popcorn around the glowing fireplace.

''He looks just like a brooding Lord Byron, wouldn't you say, honey?'' Cathleen slouched in a large leather chair, her booted feet propped on the low table in front of her.

Kelly leaned against the fireplace wall, regretting that she'd raised the subject.

"Lord who?" Dylan sounded irritable. Cathleen had forgotten to record some check stubs and he was having a devil of a time reconciling the account book with the bank statement.

"Lord Absolutely Delicious, that's who." Cathleen wasn't concerned by her new husband's foul mood. "Never mind him," she said to Kelly. "I was in the same grade as Mick, so I should know. All us girls were crazy about the guy, but he never asked any one of us out. We wondered if…well, you know, if…" She shrugged and glanced at Poppy.

The elderly woman didn't even blink. "If he was gay, you mean?"

"Yes. That's it, exactly. I've heard he spends lots of time in Calgary. Maybe he's living a double life. Respected journalist by day in Canmore, but wild drag queen by night in—"

"Knock it off, Cath!" Kelly said. Dylan had stuck his head up from the books long enough to laugh, but *she* was not amused. "Mick dates *women,* and yes, most of them have been from Calgary. So what?"

"I did hear that lately Mick has been dating Abby Stevens, the kindergarten teacher," Cathleen admitted.

Not for much longer. Kelly hoped Abby wouldn't be too disappointed when that new romance fell flat after only a couple of weeks. She felt a little bad for diverting Mick's interest, but in the long run she was certain it would be to Abby's benefit. Abby deserved to be married to someone who loved *her,* not just her child-raising skills.

And what about you, Kelly? Don't you want to marry for love one day? The irritating voice that had nagged her since her conversation with Mick last night just wouldn't shut up.

Yes, Kelly acknowledged to herself. Love and marriage were what she had once wanted for herself, too. But shooting Danny Mizzoni had changed everything. Especially now that she knew Sharon was pregnant.

One more life irrevocably affected by the events of that day. That baby would never have the opportunity to know his natural father.

How could Kelly expect the kind of normal happiness that her actions had denied to others?

"Why did you bring up Mick, anyway?" Cathleen wondered.

"Well, it's just that we're going out for pizza tomorrow night...."

"A date?"

Kelly saw the startled glance that Cathleen and Poppy exchanged. After the first ripple of surprise,

Cathleen appeared pleased, while Poppy only seemed puzzled.

No. It wasn't a date. More like a job interview. But she couldn't tell her family that. "Sort of."

"Oh, Kelly, that's great. Just the thing to stop you from moping. Only…" Now Cathleen and Dylan checked in visually with each other. "He doesn't blame you for his brother's death, does he?"

"Cath, your ability to reduce situations to their simplest denominator always astounds me."

"I'm sorry. You're right. That was kind of rude."

"But still an issue you'll need to face if you plan to see much of the man." Dylan turned off the desk lamp and came to Kelly's side. "All any of us want is to see you happy. Especially me. What you've been going through…it's all *my* fault. I know she'd fight me tooth and nail about this, but I shouldn't have taken Cathleen out to the ranch with me that day."

Neither of them should have gone to the ranch. But Kelly had given up arguing that point. She didn't blame Dylan or Cathleen for what had happened. No one could have predicted Danny's bizarre reaction.

"I appreciate your concern," she said, shaking her head as her new brother-in-law offered her a refill of her drink. "But you don't need to fuss over me. I'm just going out for pizza with Mick." *Along with his nephew and niece.*

She didn't mention that last part, though. If she was going to marry Mick, she had to get her family used to the idea gradually.

Not that they wouldn't see right through her. But she was going to do her best to pretend this was a real courtship and a real marriage. She'd thought long and hard about what Mick had said the other night. He didn't want a temporary solution, and she agreed. Billy and Amanda deserved better. When it came to family, they deserved the real thing.

Or at least a reasonable facsimile.

SELLING SHARON on letting him have the kids for the weekend hadn't been tough. She'd even permitted him to give her another lecture as part of the bargain.

"Fetal alcohol syndrome isn't the bogeyman, Sharon. This is real, serious trouble we're talking about. That baby—" he'd glanced at her still slender stomach "—could be handicapped for life with learning disabilities and behavioral problems."

"I already promised I wouldn't do any more drinking." She'd been in her housecoat, her hair a mess. Sharon was only in her mid-twenties, about five years younger than him. But she looked about ten years older. Life had been hard on her, but she'd been hard on herself, too.

"Go visit your sister in Banff," he suggested. "A change of scene might do you good." If she stayed here in this house, dwelling on her loneliness, he didn't see how she'd avoid the bottle.

Sharon looked around, as if only just becoming aware of what a disaster her home was. "I should really clean up this mess."

"I'll take care of it," he promised. Perhaps his cleaning lady would do the extra job—if he paid double. "You need to have some fun. Here, let me give you money to buy gas and to take Carrie out for a nice dinner."

He handed over a hundred-dollar bill, praying he wasn't financing another terrible drinking binge.

"A nice dinner..." Sharon sounded as confused as if he'd spoken in a foreign language.

"Sure. Get all dressed up and go to the Banff Springs Hotel for the evening. Wouldn't that be fun?"

Mick bundled the kids in their snowsuits, boots and mittens. "Say goodbye to your mom, kids. We're having a sleepover at my place."

He had a hamper of dirty clothes to take with him, plus Amanda's favorite stuffed animal, some kind of turtle, and her blankie. When he'd asked Billy if he wanted to bring anything special along, Billy just shook his head.

That had been several hours ago. Since then, he'd taken the kids for a play in the park, then brought them home to settle in before Kelly arrived at six for pizza. He got out the box of toys he kept handy for their visits, then zipped down to the basement to put in a load of laundry.

He'd left them alone for two minutes, maximum three. When he got back, they were still standing in exactly the same spot. Billy gazed longingly at the television in the corner.

"Can we watch cartoons?"

"Maybe later." Although he'd purchased a few Disney movies, he suspected they both put in too many hours in front of the television at home. "Want to make a puzzle? Or build something with these blocks?"

"Sure." Billy plopped onto the floor, his brown eyes serious.

"Which one?"

Billy shrugged.

"Okay, then. Let's do the puzzle. Want to help, Mandy?"

She, too, sat as obediently as a well-trained lapdog. Remembering what a chatterbox she'd been just months earlier, at her third birthday party, Mick felt like weeping.

The three of them put the puzzle together in silence. Mick couldn't think of anything to talk about with these small, hurting children. He wondered if they were missing their mother, but he was afraid to ask in case the answer was yes. He didn't want to return them to Sharon. If she'd taken his advice and gone to Banff, that wouldn't be an option, anyway.

By six o'clock he felt desperate. Billy and Amanda were like two well-behaved robots. He wished he could figure out what they really wanted, what they were thinking. But they seemed content to do whatever he suggested. When they finished the puzzle or the game, they just looked at him, waiting for his next suggestion.

The doorbell chiming at five minutes after six was a desperately welcome interruption. He opened the door to Kelly, who wore jeans, and a pale yellow sweatshirt under her jacket. Her hair was tied back from her face, and she carried several shopping bags.

He hung up her coat, then motioned to the living room. The kids were still sitting on the floor around a simple board game they'd been playing.

"Billy, Amanda? This is my friend Kelly. Remember, I said she'd be joining us for pizza?"

Mick could tell Kelly was nervous. She was smiling, but she'd dropped the bags and was gripping her hands behind her back.

"Hi, Billy. Hi, Amanda. Are you playing Trouble? I used to play that game with my niece."

Billy nodded, then stood. Like a shadow, Amanda followed him, taking a few steps closer to Kelly.

"I know you," Billy said suddenly.

Mick felt his heart leap against his rib cage. Sharon hadn't been clear on how much of that scene at the Thunder Bar M the kids had seen. So no one knew if Billy or his sister had witnessed Kelly shooting their father.

"Do you, Billy?" he asked, striving to sound nonchalant. He should have been smarter than to expose them to this, to take the chance of upsetting them. As if they hadn't been through enough—

"You're the lady in the car," Billy said. "Who sits and watches."

Kelly had been visibly expecting a verbal blow. This seemed to surprise her. "That's right."

"Did my daddy send you? To look out for us?"

"Oh, Billy..." Kelly angled her face toward the door, putting a hand up to veil her expression.

Mick felt bad for her. But at the moment, his nephew was his prime concern. He dropped to one knee and put his hand on the small boy's back.

"That's an interesting thought, Billy. Who knows." He glanced up at Kelly, who was rubbing away a tear with the sleeve of her yellow sweatshirt. "Maybe he did."

CHAPTER FIVE

THE TOPIC WAS DROPPED when the pizza delivery-man arrived. Perfect timing, thought Mick, for taking the pressure off the kids and Kelly.

"Where do you want to eat?" Kelly asked, as he pulled a twenty and a five from his wallet.

"In the kitchen. There's no dining room in this house. I've confiscated it for my office."

"How about I set out plates and cutlery."

They couldn't really need forks and knives for pizza, but Mick told her to go ahead. The kids stayed with him, their eyes on the fragrant cardboard box. Neither said a word, but they sure looked hungry. Maybe he should have offered them an afternoon snack.

"Okay, then," Mick said once the door was closed. "Let's go dig in."

"Should we wash our hands first?" Kelly stood in the hall off the kitchen.

"Yeah. Right." He veered toward the bathroom, and the children followed. A quick soap-up and rinse, and they were finally ready to settle around the kitchen table.

Mick pulled back the cardboard lid on the extra-large pizza. "We've got half pepperoni and cheese, half vegetarian. What kind would you like, Mandy?"

The little three-year-old said nothing—only sniffed. She had a cold or something; her nose had been running all day. Mick used a tissue to wipe her face, then shifted his gaze to Billy.

"She'll have pepperoni and cheese," Billy said. "Me, too." He turned to Kelly. "Mandy doesn't talk since our daddy went to forever."

"Oh." Kelly contemplated the little girl for a moment, then checked back with her brother. "So, how are we supposed to know what she wants?"

"Just ask me. I always know. I'm her big brother."

"She's lucky to have you, isn't she." Kelly picked up a plate, handed it to Mick for pizza, then placed it in front of Amanda. "Is this what you want Amanda?"

The little girl didn't so much as nod. But she did give a tiny smile before biting off the very tip of her slice. Beside her, Billy wiggled with impatience.

"Yours is coming, Billy," Mick said. He noticed Kelly had set out glasses of milk and a bowl of those tiny, scrubbed carrots he'd bought when he'd stocked up for the kids' visit. He watched as she offered the bowl.

"Want a carrot?"

Once Billy took one, Amanda did, too.

"I don't really like vegetables," Billy said, sniffing suspiciously.

"You might like carrots," Kelly replied. "They make a great snapping noise when you bite into them. Listen."

She bit. The carrot snapped. Amanda giggled.

"It's a little tricky to make that loud of a sound," Kelly said. "Give it a try and see if you can do it."

Mick was interested to find that both kids rose to the challenge.

"How 'bout you, Uncle Mick?" Billy asked. He was already on his third carrot.

"Oh, I'm sure I can make the loudest snap of all." Mick ground his teeth against the carrot in a sawing motion that was barely audible. Pretending to be disgusted, he took another carrot from the bowl and tried again with the same result. "This is harder than I thought—"

Crunch! The sound came from Amanda. She held up the remains of her carrot in triumph, as though to say, "Like this, Uncle Mick!"

If only the words would actually come out of her mouth. Mick had been wondering if his niece should see some kind of counselor. This not talking had been going on too long. Maybe he'd ask Kelly her opinion later. She seemed a natural with kids, but then, she'd mentioned she had a niece of her own.

That would be Maureen's daughter, he realized.

Of the three Shannon sisters, she was the one he knew the least. Not that he knew any of them all that well.

And yet, I'm thinking of marrying one. He wasn't sure when he'd begun to consider Kelly's offer seriously. At first he'd agreed to letting her meet the kids just to make her happy. But he had to admit, this was going better than he'd ever expected. So maybe it wasn't such a crazy idea, after all.

He watched Kelly chew as she carefully cut another bite-size morsel of her pizza. Her neat manners were wearing off. Both Billy and Amanda had picked up their forks. She took turns helping them with their knives.

She was a restful person to be around, so unlike her two elder sisters. Her looks matched her personality. Pretty, but in a subtle way that kind of snuck up on a person.

Catching him watching her, she gave him a rueful smile. He could interpret the slight question in her eyes. *Do I pass inspection?*

He smiled back. "Another slice of pizza?"

"No. But I'll have a second glass of milk. Anyone else?" Both children said yes.

After dinner, Mick cleaned up the kitchen. "What should we do now?" He was thinking of watching a video with the kids. It was only a few minutes after seven.

"I brought a few surprises with me," Kelly said. "Maybe we should check them out...."

"I'll get the bags," Billy volunteered, sliding out of his chair in a flash. Amanda frowned and began to struggle out of her chair, too. Mick had noticed she didn't like being separated from her brother. Not even briefly.

"He won't be long," Kelly said, also picking up on Amanda's fear.

Sure enough, Billy was already back. "Here you go—" He thrust the bags at Kelly.

She peeked into one, then passed the other to Amanda. "This is for you, sweetie. The other is for your brother."

For all his enthusiasm in bringing Kelly the bags, Billy hesitated to actually check out the contents. Amanda, as usual, took her cues from him, waiting until he'd pulled out a pair of pajamas and a picture book, before doing the same.

The pajamas were flannel, the kind with feet attached. When Amanda showed him hers, patterned with kittens, he couldn't believe how soft they were. Amanda held the fabric to his nose.

"Mmm. Smells like...like..."

"I used a special detergent for babies," Kelly said.

Yes, that was the smell. Baby-soap smell.

"I washed them in case they wanted to wear them tonight— Do you?" she asked the children.

"Sure." Billy didn't seem as impressed with the pajamas as his sister. He was pleased enough with the book, though, and had found yet a third object in the large bag.

"What's this?" He held up a small bottle.

"Oh, that's a magical bubble bath potion."

"Magical?"

"Yes. It only works after you've washed your hair." Kelly winked at Mick, and he struggled not to laugh. "Maybe we could have a bath now and try it out?"

Both kids dropped eagerly from their chairs and headed straight for the bathroom. Kelly hung back for a minute. "I hope you don't mind."

"Not at all. Good idea." In fact, by the time the kids had a bath and were read a story, it would be eight. Too late for a video, he realized.

Kelly smiled. "This is making me feel so good. Thank you for giving me this chance."

"We need the potion," Billy called from down the hall.

"Coming!" Kelly started to leave, then paused. "I mean it, Mick. Since the shooting I haven't been able to... I almost feel human again."

Mick tried to swallow. His throat barely responded. "I'm glad, Kelly," he managed to say.

"I'd better get in there, before they try to turn on the water themselves."

"Right." He walked back to the dishwasher.

She's the woman who shot my brother, he reminded himself, testing himself to see if the nerves were still raw. He could hear the water running into the tub now.

This was what normal families did every night. Sat down to meals together. Gave their young children baths, then read them stories. If it made him feel all weird and choked up, it was only because *his* home had never been like that. Neither the home he'd shared with his mother and younger brother, nor the home he'd made for himself.

But maybe he *could* make a home like that for Billy and Amanda.

And Kelly?

Could he get past the shooting? He really felt he could, that in a way he already had.

He closed his eyes, remembering her quiet, yet somehow significant, presence at the kitchen table. He tried to visualize Abby in her place, but the image wouldn't focus. Yes, Abby was sweet and chatty; and yes, Abby loved children.

But substituting her for Kelly threw the entire picture off balance.

A TOUCH OF DISHARMONY had been inevitable, Kelly told herself. It occurred at bedtime, after stories, when Billy asked to phone his mother.

"Your mom went to Banff to visit her sister," Mick explained. "I'll get the phone number, but don't be disappointed if they aren't home. I believe they were planning to go out to dinner.''

Kelly sat on the edge of Billy's bed. Across the room, Amanda slept curled around her blankie and special turtle. Billy, with his droopy eyelids and big yawns, had seemed poised to follow his sister's example only minutes ago. However, thoughts of his mother had worked like adrenaline. Now he bouncing nervously on the mattress.

''But dinner is over.''

Mick came into the room, holding the receiver of his portable phone. ''No answer, buddy. I'm sorry.''

Billy's bright eyes overflowed.

Kelly put an arm around his thin shoulders. ''You'll see her in a day or two—''

''No!'' He jerked away and reached, instead, for his uncle. ''She's gone, isn't she.''

''No, Billy.'' Mick's arms easily engulfed the small boy. ''Your mom is okay and she'll be coming home again.''

He was so patient with the children, Kelly had noticed. A little clueless in some areas, such as baths and tuck-in procedures, but definitely his heart was in the right place. She could see his mouth working whenever someone asked Amanda a question, as if trying to put the words in her mouth for her.

Now she could tell he ached for Billy. Maybe it was too soon for the children to be separated from their mother. But to feed them a decent meal, to wash them properly and read them stories had been so wonderful.

If Mick hadn't believed her earlier that the care they were receiving from Sharon was not up to par, watching them in the bath would certainly have changed his mind. Amanda had a rash on her bum that Kelly was certain was due to poor hygiene, and without clothes it was clear the children were both too thin.

At a nod from Mick, Kelly left the room. To calm the distraught child didn't take him long. Fifteen minutes later, he joined her in the living room. She'd pulled a book from the shelves and had put her feet up and begun to read a true account of a disastrous climbing expedition on Mount Everest. Fascinating as the tale promised to be, she set the hardcover aside easily to question Mick.

"Is he okay?"

"Yeah. He's asleep." Mick looked as though *he* hadn't slept in about a week. He went to the big front window, checked the blind. Was he worried about the neighbors seeing them together? She knew he had his reservations about their...partnership. Had tonight improved her odds? She'd thought so, until that little scene with Billy.

"I don't think he misses his mom so much as he's concerned about her," he elaborated. "If she gets sick, who'll care for her? He's afraid she might have forgotten the pills that make her head feel better, or the drinks that help her sore throat." He raised his eyebrows ironically.

"Oh." The reality of Billy's situation slammed home. "That poor child."

"Are you talking about Billy? Or the unborn baby?"

"Both. And Sharon, too. Much as I hate what she's doing to these kids, she so obviously needs help."

"I know. I'm hoping her sister can help her pull herself together."

"What's she like?"

"Carrie?" Mick settled on the sofa across from Kelly's chair. When he put his feet up on the table, only a few inches separated his toes from hers. He didn't seem to notice, but suddenly Kelly was very conscious about not moving.

"She's okay. A few years younger than Sharon, and single. She holds a steady job."

"Even if she was a trained therapist, expecting her to straighten out Sharon in one weekend is a little much to hope for, don't you think?"

"Oh, I know it." Mick sighed, then sat up straight. "Want a drink or anything? Sorry I didn't offer sooner."

"No drink, thanks, but coffee or tea would be nice. I can do it. Which would you prefer?"

But Mick was already standing. "I usually drink coffee. But I can make tea...."

"Coffee would be wonderful," she assured him. Once he left the room she closed her eyes, relaxed and reflected. Observing Mick at home, with the children, had been an education. Their warm relationship was obvious, but she wondered if she was the only one who sensed an invisible barrier around Mick that even the kids weren't permitted past.

Some might have interpreted this as coldness, but that wasn't true. Mick cared about people, and he was thoughtful. The reserve had to be part of his personality.

"Milk, right?" Mick was back with two mugs in his hands.

"Yes, thanks." How easily two people could slide into a set routine, she thought. From just the previous night, he remembered how she took her coffee. If that was all marriage was—the merging of two separate lifestyles into one—neither she nor Mick would be hard-pressed to adapt.

Yet, that wasn't all marriage was—or at least, ought to be.

"Have you given any consideration to what we— we talked about the other night?" she asked.

"I have. And I admit the idea has merits. Especially after tonight. You seem pretty knowledgeable about kids...."

His comment trailed off into the quiet of the evening. Not a peep had been heard from the children's room since Billy had fallen asleep. The dishwasher had finished its cycle. Kelly could close her eyes and imagine she was all alone. But that wasn't what she wanted. Because it was when she was alone that her demons attacked most ferociously.

"But have you considered whether you could live with me, given what happened...what I've done?"

She'd been afraid to bring up the issue. But where once Mick had displayed such passionate anger, now he was amazingly calm.

"Kelly, I've read all the statements, talked to witnesses and to Springer. You reacted that day exactly as you'd been trained to. Springer said he couldn't have asked more from one of his officers."

"Yeah." She'd heard all this so many times. From Springer, from her colleagues and most especially from her sisters. They all wanted to absolve her from guilt. Only Poppy seemed to understand it wasn't that simple. Kelly was a person before she was an RCMP officer. Rules and regulations notwithstanding, she had to take responsibility for what she'd done.

"I admit I was badly shaken up at first," he said. "But I like to think I'm a reasonable person. My journalism training has conditioned me to see both sides of an issue. When I feel angry these days, it's mostly at Danny."

"Were you and your brother close?"

"I was five years older. I've spent my life trying to watch out for him. Didn't do much of a job."

"Why do you say that?"

"Isn't it obvious? Look at what happened...."

"I don't see how any of it is *your* fault."

"I just wish I could understand what was in his head. Danny had a good job and a home for his family. Why did he need to get involved with drugs again? And what was he doing with an illegal gun in the first place?"

Kelly wished she could say something to comfort Mick. But what she'd found these past few months was that there were layers to pain. And the deeper ones just couldn't be reached by words.

Instinctively, she went to sit beside him, reaching an arm over his shoulder. It was the first time she'd ever touched Mick Mizzoni.

She didn't say, *It'll be okay,* because she knew it never would be. Danny's death was a cold, hard fact.

Mick, head bowed, took a few deep breaths. She felt the tension ebb in the muscles across his back. His wool sweater was thick and soft, and she fought an urge to lean her face against it.

"You okay?" she asked, keeping her voice gentle.

He nodded, raising his head. "Sure." He eased her arm from his shoulders and took her hand in his. Gently he kissed her knuckles, then brought his gaze up to her face.

"You've just reminded me of something else we need to talk about," he said.

"Oh?"

"Sex."

Her heart felt as if it had jumped six inches in her chest. "Pardon me?"

His gaze lowered to her hand again. She noticed the way his longish hair fell in waves back from his face, and unexpectedly she thought of her sister's comparison to Lord Byron. In some ways, it wasn't far off.

"If we go ahead with this marriage idea..." he began.

"Yes?"

"I told you it would have to be real. That includes the bit about 'forsaking all others.' And I don't plan on a life of celibacy."

"Which, of course, means that you and I..." She couldn't look at him now. Mature adults that they both were, the conversation was too bizarre. Making love with Mick would be no hardship. But planning and discussing for the possibility was just too embarrassing. Yet Mick didn't seem at all shy.

"Yes. Eventually. What I'm trying to say is that we might find it more comfortable to wait a while until we know each other better."

Kelly wasn't so happy to hear that. Her female pride, she realized, would have preferred to hear that he really didn't think he was capable of waiting. But she was forgetting the real reason for the marriage.

"Does this mean that you've decided we should go ahead?"

Finally, he allowed himself a small smile. "Yes. And quickly. I can't have you staying here otherwise. It wouldn't look right to the community. More important, it wouldn't be the proper thing for Billy and Amanda."

"I understand." Or did she? Suddenly the situation was spinning out of control. Tonight, she'd hoped to persuade Mick to consider her plan. Never had she expected he would buy into it so readily.

"I'll start organizing the paperwork on Monday."

"Yes…" She tried to gauge her emotions. This was what she'd thought she wanted. Reviewing the evening she'd just spent, she acknowledged it was what she still wanted. Seeing those children happy was the only hope in her life right now. Even as she recovered emotionally, she knew that tie between them would never be broken.

"This is good, Mick. I have one question, though."

He waited.

"What if Sharon eventually does pull herself together?"

"Realistically, I'm not sure that's ever going to happen. Understand—I've known Sharon much longer than you have. But if she does, I'd be the last one to want to keep her from her children."

"In which case our…partnership…"

"Would be over. But only if the kids don't need us."

She nodded. "Yes, I agree, Mick. Let's get married as quickly as we can."

The relief in Mick's eyes was a sweet tonic to the unexpected sadness she'd begun to feel.

"This hasn't been the most romantic courtship," he conceded. "But we'll make good partners. I've always admired… That is, there's a peacefulness about you that I've always found attractive."

So easily, Kelly could imagine her sister Cathleen's reply if a man dared make a comment like that after his proposal: *Yes, but don't you find me sexy?*

Cathleen could get away with questions like that, because she obviously *was*. But Kelly couldn't. Besides, lately sex had been the last thing on her mind.

Until today. Tonight. When Mick had kissed her knuckles, she'd found herself longing for those kisses to travel upward. So what did that mean? Not much, she decided. Mick was an extremely attractive guy, and she was feeling emotionally stronger than she had in months. Her reactions were the normal, physical response of a healthy female.

To a man who was soon to become her husband.

CHAPTER SIX

BILLY AWOKE to the sound of crying. At first he thought it was his mom again. But after a few moments with his eyes open, he remembered he was at his uncle Mick's and that Amanda wasn't in the bed with him. He sat up.

"Mandy?" There was a small, trembling bump at the bottom of her bed. He went to check it out. Sure enough, the bump was his sister, huddled into a ball underneath all her covers.

He pulled away the quilt, and the wailing became louder.

"Did you wet the bed again?"

Just more crying.

Gosh, but it was annoying. Billy went to the light switch by the door and turned it on. He rubbed his eyes for a few moments, then went out into the hall. Which way to Uncle Mick's room? He had to think a few seconds before he remembered.

There was a night-light in the bathroom—in case they woke up and had to go. Too bad it hadn't worked.

Farther down the hall, he heard snoring. It

sounded just like his daddy, and he felt a buzz of excitement. He pushed the door and checked, but it was only Uncle Mick, lying on his back, his mouth slightly open.

Billy moved closer, wondering if Uncle Mick was grouchy when he woke up. Would he be mad at Billy for disturbing him? Turned out he didn't have to worry, though.

"What?" Uncle Mick opened his eyes. He seemed a little surprised to have Billy staring right at his face. "You okay, Billy? Thought I heard—"

"*Waahhhh!*" Amanda was totally freaking out now.

Uncle Mick jumped out of bed and ran. Billy followed.

"SWEETHEART, WHAT IS IT? Did you have a nightmare?" Mick had Amanda in his arms by the time Billy was back in the room.

He watched his little nephew—adorable in his new pajamas, with his hair sticking up at the back of his head—cross his arms and pronounce with the assurance of a seasoned doctor.

"Probably wet her bed. She does that most nights."

"But—" Mick remembered a previous time he'd had the children to stay so Danny and Sharon could go away for the weekend. He was sure Sharon had told him Mandy no longer needed diapers. Then it clicked.

"You mean since your dad…"

Billy nodded.

"Okay. Well, that's good to know. Come on, sweetie. We'll put you in something dry, then get these sheets changed. Billy, you hop back into bed."

"I can help."

"Yes, I know, but you must be tired. I'll take care of this. Okay, Mandy?"

His little niece was calm now that he was holding her close. She *was* very wet, though. He wondered if the situation called for a bath.

Kelly would know. She'd automatically told them to wash their hands before dinner—a little thing that hadn't occurred to him. Then, when she'd suggested baths and stories, he'd realized how much of parenting he had no clue about.

He'd never learned any of those things from his childhood. The idea of his mother asking him to wash his hands before a meal was enough to make him laugh. Actually bothering to prepare a meal was something his mother had rarely done.

Mick had learned about manners and social norms from watching television, reading books and observing other families from a distance. Of course, that had left gaps in his education.

Gently, he carried the little girl to the bathroom. She was shivering with cold. Yet still so sleepy she kept her eyes closed. To force her into the tub seemed cruel. He decided to wipe her off with a washcloth, then dress her quickly in a pair of sweatpants and a shirt of Billy's.

"That feel better?" he asked when he was done.

She smiled and curled into his pillow. He hadn't known where else to put her. He didn't own a spare set of sheets. After watching her for several minutes, he gave in to his fatigue and settled on the opposite side of the bed.

At some point in the night, he awoke to find Amanda curled right next to him, like a puppy.

So sweet, he thought, stroking her cheek. Her lips fluttered briefly, but her eyelids stayed firmly closed. *Give me the chance,* he prayed, *and I'll be a good father.*

But would he have the opportunity? Sharon would be home again in two or three days. He'd already decided that he was going to ask if she would let the kids stay with him a little longer. He had no idea how she would react to the idea. Or to finding out that he and Kelly were getting married on Wednesday.

"LET'S SEE if I've got this straight." Cathleen was sitting across from Kelly and Maureen at the Bagel Bites Café. "You've had one date with Mick Mizzoni—*one date!*—and now you want to get married?"

Oh, how she'd dreaded this conversation. Kelly glanced at her eldest sister without much hope of finding support from that quarter. Sure enough, Maureen's frown of disapproval reminded her of their mother's expression when she found out about one of Cathleen's pranks.

"This isn't like you, Kelly. You're normally so practical and careful. Definitely not impulsive...."

"This is beyond impulsive, Maureen. It's insanity! Obviously we need to switch counselors. I know Scott Martin came recommended by the department, but I'm sure we can find—"

"Forget it." Kelly slammed a hand on the wooden table, shaking all three coffee cups. Maureen used a napkin to soak up the spills. "This decision isn't about counseling *or* Scott."

"Of course not. It's about the kids," Maureen said.

"The kids?" Cathleen threw her hands up in the air. "What kids? Have both of you lost your minds? I thought we were talking about Kelly and Mick Miz—" She paused, then lowered her voice several decibels. "Oh, I see. Danny's kids. Is *that* why you're doing this, Kel?"

"If so, it's a big mistake," Maureen continued. "I hate to sound like the mean big sister here, but you know marriage is serious business."

"Heavenly, with the right person," Cathleen said.

She and Dylan were definitely still in the blissful stage.

"But agony with Mr. Wrong," said Maureen. Her experiences with Rod had definitely been disillusioning.

"This is so strange. Usually *I'm* the one lecturing you two."

"That's partly why I'm so worried," Maureen replied. "You still haven't recovered from Danny's shooting. You're not yourself. Even if you and Mick had been dating for a year, this wouldn't be the right time to make life-altering decisions."

But in terms of Billy's and Amanda's welfare, it was exactly the right time. The only time. She hadn't told her sisters about Sharon's negligence with the kids. They would insist on calling Child Welfare, which would be an absolute disaster. The kids' uncle was ready and willing to help. All he needed was a partner. And she fully intended to be the one.

"Only last week," Cathleen reminded her, "Mick was dating Abby Stevens!"

Kelly decided she'd had enough. "Look, I'm sorry if I gave you the wrong impression about this meeting. I didn't ask you here to *discuss* my plans for the future. I'm *telling* you. Mick and I are getting married. It's happening Wednesday evening at his house. You can come...or not."

Confrontations, especially with her family, had

never been her strong suit. By nature she was a conciliator, at work as well as at home. But her sisters weren't talking her out of this. Kelly hid her trembling hands in her lap. She hoped her voice had sounded firm and confident. It must have. Neither Maureen nor Cathleen spoke for a good sixty seconds.

Finally, Cathleen gave a quavering smile. "Need a bridesmaid?"

Maureen reached across the table to give her a hug. "I'll bring the champagne."

IN SOME WAYS, informing Poppy about her upcoming wedding was even harder than telling her sisters. Poppy understood so much more, which only meant she posed tougher questions.

"Are you sure this is better for the children? As husband and wife you and Mick might offer a stable home life. But children are masters at seeing through deception. A fake marriage isn't going to fool them."

They were at the kitchen table. Dylan and Cathleen, along with the two other couples who were staying at the B and B that night, had already retired to their rooms. Poppy had made the usual cocoa and muffins. For a change, Kelly found she had an appetite.

Both eating and sleeping had come easier to her since she and Mick had decided to get married. A sign, she was certain, that she was making the right choice.

"It won't be fake, Poppy. Mick told me right from the beginning that he's only interested in a real marriage. We've just skipped the courtship stage, that's all."

And Kelly didn't feel she was marrying a total stranger. She and Mick had both lived in Canmore all their lives—except for Kelly's RCMP training and her first couple of postings in northern Saskatchewan. During those years they'd been acquaintances at best—but there was something about knowing each other's history….

Kelly was aware Mick's early years had been rough. But he'd excelled in university, and his work at the *Canmore Leader* was widely respected. His immaculate home and his love for his niece and nephew boded well for his having a sense of commitment and feeling of responsibility.

"The children will grow up and leave eventually. What then?"

"We haven't thought *that* far ahead, Poppy."

"Well, maybe you should. You're tying yourself to this man for *life*."

Again, Poppy's point was more than valid. But Kelly still felt not a shred of doubt that she wasn't doing the right thing. "Mick is a good man. In fact, I think he's an even better man than he knows."

"Ah." Poppy sounded as if she'd found something significant in Kelly's comment, but when she spoke it was about the children again.

"If the kids weren't part of the picture, would you still consider marrying him?"

The first answer that occurred to her was, *Of course not.* The pang of disappointment that immediately followed that thought, however, forced her to question herself. She'd been attracted to Mick before, had wished he might ask her out one day. Perhaps she'd wished that a little more than she'd ever admitted to herself.

"It wouldn't be out of the question, Poppy. But the kids certainly cinch matters. In some cultures, if you save a person's life that person becomes your responsibility for the rest of *your* life."

"I've heard that."

"Well, don't you think the responsibility becomes that much more onerous if you *take* someone's life? A long-term commitment to Danny's children feels right to me." Oddly enough, marrying Mick did, too.

Kelly had a last bite of muffin and washed it down with half a mug of cocoa. It was time for her to head home—no longer the dismal prospect it had once been.

At the door, Poppy's final words were accepting. "Let me bake some appetizers for the wedding, Kelly. I'm honored you thought to invite me."

MICK WONDERED how Kelly was making out, breaking the news of their upcoming wedding to her family. He'd offered to come with her, to present a united front, but she'd refused—and she was probably right. No doubt her family wouldn't be thrilled that she was marrying a boy from the wrong side of town.

Which he most certainly was. The teasing and tormenting he'd endured during his school years had left him in no doubt of his ranking in the social order of Canmore. He wasn't naive enough to think that four years of university and a career at the *Leader* had changed anyone's underlying opinion about his worth.

Although the Shannons hadn't exactly been wealthy themselves, their family had definitely been respected and well-liked. He was certain none of them would think very highly of this marriage.

Maybe it would be for the best if they talked Kelly out of it. He would be in a bit of a bind—especially since he'd already broken off with Abby—but he'd find a solution.

Until Kelly told him she was backing out, though, he was carrying on with their plans. So far he'd arranged for a justice of the peace and obtained their marriage license. The next step was to fill Sharon in on the news. He didn't anticipate she'd be thrilled. He was afraid, in fact, that she might throw a fit.

He'd arranged a sitter for Amanda and Billy for

Monday morning, so he could go to work. Sharon was supposed to be back from Banff around noon, and his plan was to drop the kids off with her for a few hours, then pick them up at dinnertime.

At one o'clock, his phone rang. Mick turned from his computer so he could see out the window. The view of the mountains always helped put the problems of this world into perspective. As soon as he heard Sharon's voice, he knew he was going to need all the patience he could muster.

"Miggie?"

His stomach tightened. "Sharon, is that you?"

"Sssure is. I'm home. Where're the kids?"

Just past noon and she was already drunk. He just couldn't believe it. "They're at a sitter's. Have a shower, Sharon. I'm coming over to talk."

"I want my babies...." she whined.

Not in my lifetime. "I'll be there in five minutes."

Mick saved the computerized version of the editorial he'd been working on, then called out to the office receptionist that he'd be gone for an hour or two. On the way to the bungalow he phoned the sitter and arranged for her to stay on until he was able to get home.

At Sharon's he had to knock loudly, and several times, before he heard her call out for him to come in. He opened the side door and glanced around the kitchen. It was still pristine from the cleaning he'd arranged over the weekend, however, an odor of burning coffee mingled with the familiar scent of cleaning products. He took off his shoes before walking across the shining linoleum floor to turn off the machine.

"Just out of the shower," Sharon called again. "Hang on a minute."

She emerged a few seconds later in a robe, her hair gathered up in a towel. She had a coffee mug in one hand and a smile of greeting on her face. The smile fell flat almost immediately.

"Where're the kids?"

"With a sitter," he reminded her. The shower appeared to have done some good. She was steady on her feet and her voice was back to normal. But her eyes were puffy, red and bloodshot. From crying or drinking? he wondered. Or both?

"How was your visit with your sister?"

"Not bad. We went out for dinner like you suggested. Then we went dancing…" She'd put her hands to her belly protectively and turned away from him. "Don't look at me that way. I needed to have a little fun."

"I don't even know what to say to that, Sharon."

"For a change, don't say anything. And sit down, why don't you. You're making me nervous pacing the way you are."

He waited until Sharon had settled into one of the kitchen chairs before seating himself at the table opposite from her. He watched as she removed the towel from her head and commenced to finger-comb her wet hair. She'd had it cut while she was gone—into short spiky layers. The new style emphasized her gauntness and her large brown eyes.

"I'm glad you stopped by," she said. "I need to tell you something before you give me my lecture."

At his silence, she raised her eyebrows. "I assume that's why you came here. So you could preach about the evils of smoking and drinking."

Mick shook his head. "Actually, no. It's... something else."

"Yeah? Well, that sounds interesting." She tapped her fingernails on the tabletop anxiously, and that was when he noticed the package of cigarettes sitting behind the sugar bowl.

He looked from the cigarettes back to Sharon. She forestalled his objection.

"Hold the lecture, Mickey. I know smoking is bad for the kid. I won't have more than one or two a day."

What could he say? "Is that your news?"

"Of course not. The thing is, I met someone this weekend." Sharon adjusted the position of the sugar bowl, then arranged the salt and pepper shakers on either side. "I hope this doesn't shock you, 'cause I did love Danny, but he's gone now—and being on my own hasn't been easy."

His brother had been dead little over two months! Mick was shocked, but didn't figure it would pay to show it. If Sharon needed a crutch to get through the pain of Danny's death, he'd rather it was another guy than booze and drugs.

"A good guy?" he asked.

"Who knows?" Sharon covered her mouth and coughed before continuing. "Brian works at Melissa's Steakhouse and he's a terrific dancer. That's enough for now."

"Oh."

"Anyway, I was thinking of going back to Banff and staying with my sister awhile. She said it would be okay."

"What about Billy and Amanda?"

"They like Carrie."

He couldn't let this happen. How could he watch over the children if they were in Banff...twenty minutes farther along the Trans-Canada Highway? "You could leave the kids with me, Sharon. I'm always happy to have them."

"Really?" Sharon's expression lifted enough for him to realize this was what she'd been hoping for. "Well, Carrie's place is pretty small. It might not be a bad idea."

Relief loosened the hard knot in his gut. "There's something I have to tell you before you go." He decided just to blurt it out. "I'm getting married."

"What?" Sharon dropped her hands flat to the table and stared. "You never even told us you had a girlfriend."

"Well, it's someone I've known for a long time."
He fought the urge to get up and start moving again.
"Actually, it's Kelly Shannon."

"That lady cop who shot Danny? You're kidding,
right?"

"I guess it must seem strange, but you've got to
understand that what happened to Danny wasn't her
fault. Any cop who showed up at that scene
would've reacted the same way."

"She killed your own brother…. This doesn't
make any sense!" Sharon pushed against the table
as she stood. Leaning over him, she shook her fist.
"Damn it, Mickey, tell me you're not serious!"

He abandoned his chair and moved to the counter
by the back window. Fresh snow crowned the spruce
trees that stood along the property line. They
dwarfed the house and the backyard, and cut off any
view of the mountains to the north.

Sharon continued ranting. She cursed Kelly's
name, questioned his sanity, then finally grew calm.

"You're really going to do this?"

He nodded. "Wednesday."

"Oh my God, so soon?"

"It's what we want. No point in waiting."

"I guess not."

He heard the sound of running water, Sharon
opening a cupboard for a glass. Finally he faced her
again, watching as she drank. When she was done,
she wiped her mouth with the back of her hand.

"I wonder how the kids will feel about this. Have you told them?"

"Not yet."

"I suppose you won't have as much time to spend with them anymore...."

"Not true. I'll always have time for Billy and Amanda."

"Maybe I should take them with me after all."

"No, Sharon." God, perhaps he shouldn't have told her about his wedding plans. But she had to know eventually.

"You don't understand. I need my babies."

But what about *their* needs? Mick didn't want his niece and nephew back in her care, not until she was sober and responsible. "What about this new guy you met? This'll give you a chance to get to know him."

"Well..."

"Plus, you could use a break from the routine of looking after children. You're exhausted. And you have to start eating properly. You haven't eaten any breakfast, have you."

"Sure I have."

His gaze swept the pristine counters. Only the coffee machine appeared to have been touched since the cleaning lady had been there.

"I guess three cups of coffee doesn't qualify as breakfast in your opinion."

"Get dressed. I'll take you to my place. You can

visit with the kids and I'll make you something, before you come back to pack for Banff.''

Fingering the belt on her robe, Sharon sighed. ''Will *she* be there?''

''Kelly? No. I have a neighbor lady in with the kids.''

''Well…okay, then. I'll just be a second.'' She waited until he was rinsing out her coffee cup, though, before she turned to go. He could guess why she'd waited.

''Leave the cigarettes on the table, Sharon.''

''Damn you, Mick. You're worse than my mother ever was.''

As he rinsed out the coffee machine, again Mick wondered if he was doing the right thing. Sharon's antipathy toward Kelly, although understandable, might create problems for him and Kelly later.

But with his limited options, he didn't see any way around the problem. Sharon was just going to have to accept Kelly as his wife. Which she probably would do with her usual grace and aplomb.

Right.

CHAPTER SEVEN

KELLY MET MICK at his house at five o'clock on Wednesday. The wedding was scheduled for seven. Poppy had insisted on taking the children to the B and B so the couple could have a few hours of quiet before the ceremony.

Kelly wasn't normally too fussy about clothing. She'd worn a uniform to work for most of her adult life. On weekends she favored sportswear appropriate for running and skiing and hiking in the mountains. But for this wedding, her sisters hadn't let her get away with a shrug. First they'd tried to insist on a dress. She'd held firm. But when Maureen brought down a pantsuit she'd seen in a new boutique in Calgary, Kelly had felt it would be churlish to refuse.

Now she smoothed her hands down the sides of the silk trousers. The silver buttons on the matching taupe jacket picked up the sparkles in the camisole that had come with the outfit. Cathleen had insisted she wear their mother's pearls—Cathleen had worn them for her own wedding—as well as heels.

Kelly felt as if she were dressed for an undercover

assignment. She knocked at Mick's door apprehensively. Would he think she'd gone over the top for what was supposed to be a simple home ceremony?

But Mick's eyes spelled only appreciation when he opened the door to her.

"You look...lovely."

So did he. As though he'd planned his wardrobe to coordinate with hers, he had on a gray turtleneck, dress pants and a navy blazer. His dark hair had been brushed so the waves obediently fell from his face, making it easy to focus on his compelling, dark green eyes with their thick frame of lashes.

"Mick, you're—" She felt too shy to give him the compliment she'd been thinking. Immediately she saw the absurdity of that. How could she marry a man she didn't feel comfortable with?

And yet, she wasn't excessively nervous about her decision. She kept expecting it to happen—a fit of shaking, an impulse to run. But she remained relatively calm and collected. Her sisters were the ones who'd been going crazy these past few days.

"Come sit down." Mick took her hand in his. She marveled that they both had such cool, dry palms. "Want a drink?"

"A little wine, maybe."

Before he'd even made it to the kitchen, however, the doorbell rang. It was a local florist, with two huge arrangements, a bouquet of white roses and a matching boutonniere.

"Must be my sisters," Kelly explained as she helped Mick pin on the boutonniere. "I've tried to tell them we just want something small and simple, but they've insisted on turning this into a real wedding. Poppy's been cooking for days, and Maureen's arranged for some music...."

Mick brushed a strand of fern from her lapel. "That's okay, isn't it? Didn't you ever dream of your wedding day when you were a young girl?"

"Not really. I remember watching Princess Diana and Prince Charles's extravaganza with my mother and thinking it seemed like torture."

Mick laughed. "Well, I hope you won't find the next three or four hours quite that painful." He disappeared into the kitchen and came back with two flutes.

"Is champagne okay?" He touched his glass to hers. "To real weddings and real marriages."

Kelly took one sip and then another. Mick was being so sweet, but in a few hours, when they said their vows to each other, his brother wouldn't be there to act as his best man. Kelly wished she could tell him how sorry she felt about that, but coming from her, the comment would hardly be appropriate.

She moved to the fireplace, pretending to admire the arrangements they'd placed on the hearth. "Have you heard from Sharon?"

"Last night she called the kids. From the background noise it was obvious she was at a bar." Mick fussed with the cushions on the sofa. "Maybe I should've tried to convince her to stay in Canmore. I'd hoped her sister would be a good influence, but she's obviously not."

"Just because Sharon was in a bar doesn't mean she had to be drinking."

"Kelly, an alcoholic like Sharon can't be in a bar and not drink."

"Well, that's her choice, isn't it? Even if she was still living here, you wouldn't be able to stop her."

"Yeah, I know, but I feel so damn guilty. I'm looking after Billy and Amanda, sure. But what about that poor, unborn child? I've done research into fetal alcohol syndrome, Kelly. I'm sure my brother suffered from it. Fortunately both Billy and Amanda seem to be okay, but this new baby… God, I don't see how it stands a chance. The first months are the most important, and I'll bet there hasn't been a day since…well, since Danny died, that Sharon hasn't had a drink."

Which placed the responsibility squarely back on Kelly's shoulders.

"I'm sorry, Kelly. I didn't mean to blame Sharon's drinking on you."

"It's okay. I understand…" Mick's arm at her waist was undoubtedly meant to be comforting, but she reacted to his touch in a decidedly sexual way. Which made her think of their upcoming night together and Mick's comment about waiting until they were *comfortable* before moving into the same bedroom. Since Billy and Amanda slept together, there was a third room available for her. Her clothes were already in the closet and the four-drawer bureau.

Subleasing her basement apartment and getting rid of the items she had no further need for—that would happen later. Suddenly, she wasn't sure she was ready for that. She slipped out from under Mick's arm and went to lean against the fireplace wall. She was becoming subsumed by this marriage. Not by Mick's intention, but because it seemed most reasonable to move into *his* house, to use *his* furniture and *his* belongings.

"Getting nervous?"

Mick was too perceptive, and she didn't know how to answer him. She certainly wasn't about to change her mind. The doorbell saved her from having to respond. It was the trio of musicians. Wanting time to get a feel for the place and to tune their instruments, they'd arrived early. No sooner had their needs been accommodated, however, than Poppy arrived in her Tracker with the food. Fifteen minutes later, Cathleen, Dylan, Maureen and her daughter, Holly, showed up with the kids, and about a dozen helium-filled balloons.

"Holly insisted on stopping for these," Maureen explained, transferring a handful of trailing ribbons to Billy and Amanda before giving Kelly a peck on the cheek and a hug.

"It wouldn't be a party without balloons. Right, kids?"

Next, Kelly gave her niece a big squeeze. She and Holly had always been close. But Holly had pulled inward after her father's death. Now, even though her mood was cheerful, it had a forced quality that Kelly saw right through.

"You okay?" she whispered.

Holly wouldn't look at her. "Sure." She turned to the little kids. "You can let go of the ribbons now, guys. See what happens."

Billy watched his share of the balloons pop right up to the ceiling. "Wow!" Beside him, Amanda held tightly to her brightly colored ribbons.

Someone—probably Maureen—had gone crazy with Amanda, curling her hair and dressing her in a beautiful velvet smock. Billy was wearing nothing special, but his play clothes were clean and his hair brushed. Kelly was glad no one had forced the small boy to get all dressed up. She bent at the knee to ask him if he'd made out okay at the B and B.

"They have horses," he said, awestruck. "Did you know Dylan is a real, live cowboy?"

"Sure. He used to ride bulls in the rodeo. And he works as the foreman for one of the biggest ranches in Alberta."

One day Dylan hoped to ranch his own land again. He'd asked Maureen to look into possibly challenging his mother's will, which had left the Thunder Bar M to her husband, Max.

"Cathleen let me ride her horse. And Poppy made us cookies.... I like your family, Kelly."

"After this wedding, they'll be your family, too."

"Really?"

She nodded. *Really.* Yet another reminder of what marriage was. So much more than just the joining of two individuals. She was thankful her sisters and their families had been so welcoming to Billy and Amanda. She had no doubt they would treat them with all the love and affection they showered on Maureen's Holly.

God knows, Billy and Amanda could use the attention.

"Ready?" Cathleen passed her the rose bouquet. The justice of the peace stood by the fireplace, and the musicians made a smooth transition into a bridal march. This was it.

Kelly clutched her flowers.

"You don't have to go through with it," Cathleen whispered.

Kelly shook her head. Her sister didn't understand. She was desperate to have this ceremony take place, desperate to offer Billy and Amanda all the comfort and security she had to give.

And there, in front of the fireplace, stood the man who was making this possible for her. Mick didn't appear at all nervous. His eyes were on her as stead-

fastly as if he were a normal groom, in love with
the woman he was about to marry.

Love. That, too, was what marriage was about.
And didn't they have an abundance? Already, she
loved Billy and Amanda, as of course did Mick.
As for loving Mick, that would likely come in time.

She let his gaze center her as she covered the
distance between them. At the end, he held out his
arm and she took it, not breaking the visual connection between them.

As the justice of the peace began to speak, Kelly
saw the pupils of Mick's eyes grow darker and bigger. She stood, transfixed, as the words washed over
her, some so familiar she barely heard them, others
so poignant it was like the first time she'd heard
them spoken.

They exchanged vows. Then rings. Mick had
bought a matching set of platinum bands. She tightened her grip on his arm in the moment before he
kissed her. And the truth hit her like the shower of
petals Holly tossed after the justice pronounced
them man and wife.

She was already in love.

KELLY HAD TO GIVE her family credit. She'd sprung
an incredibly hasty wedding on them, and after their
initial shock, they'd reacted with grace. The congratulations and celebrations after the short service
couldn't have been more genuine or touching.

Everyone had to take a turn at making a toast. First Maureen, then Cathleen and finally Dylan. Poppy hustled in the kitchen, serving tray after tray of beautiful appetizers: tiny Yorkshire puddings stuffed with roast beef and horseradish, pineapple-glazed shrimp, three-cheese roll-ups and spinach puffs.

Billy and Amanda loved the commotion and all the attention. Kelly tossed Amanda her bouquet after the service, and Poppy enlisted Billy's help in carrying around trays. He took the job seriously, carefully balancing the plates of food and making sure not to exclude anyone in his offerings.

"Isn't Billy cute?" Kelly asked Mick, after they'd cut the delicately frosted cake that Poppy had also contributed. "He's so serious. When I told him he could take a break, he refused."

"Billy likes having a job to do. I've noticed that about him. Watch him with Amanda—how he takes care of her."

"Yes, I know." Kelly glanced at her husband, instead. *Husband.* She imagined that as a boy of five, he'd probably been a lot like Billy. Instead of caring for a younger sister, though, he'd had Danny to contend with.

From all accounts, Danny had been a handful right from the start, with a short attention span and uncontrollable emotional swings. Perhaps it was the fetal alcohol syndrome Mick had mentioned earlier.

"Your family is wonderful. I couldn't believe all the speeches."

"Unfortunately, it's hard to shut them up once they get started."

"I can't imagine wanting to do that. Did you really suspect Maureen's first boyfriend of being a serial murderer?"

Kelly wished Maureen had kept quiet about that particular escapade. "You have to understand, I was an undercover detective from the age of nine. Intriguing crimes were hard to come by. I had to be inventive."

"What a kid you must have been."

"Funny, I was just thinking that about you."

"Really?"

"Yes, when I was watching Billy."

"Danny always said he'd produced a clone of me." Mick's affectionate smile faded.

Perhaps thoughts of his brother were just too painful. Once more, Kelly longed to tell him how sorry she was, but the warm moment between them had faded.

Mick touched her lightly on the elbow. "I should check if Amanda's gone to the bathroom recently. When she's excited, she sometimes forgets."

"Sure." Kelly knew she was foolish for feeling bereft as he moved away. The illogical reaction reminded her of how she'd felt during their wedding ceremony. Mick said he intended for their marriage to be real, but she was certain he had no idea how shockingly strong her feelings were for him. Almost overnight she'd gone from a distant admiration to a passionate, almost wild infatuation.

She'd stepped into this marriage with open eyes, anticipating that over the long term love would develop. Not the head-over-heels kind, but a mature affection that would arise from compatible personalities, shared interests and common history.

Never had she expected that in less than a week, she'd find herself constantly thinking of him, wanting to be with him, craving physical attention from him.

But the kiss that had bound them for life had been their first. And Kelly had no idea when she might expect a second.

Noticing Maureen about to descend on her, she gave a quick excuse about helping Poppy and fled the living room. She found Poppy washing trays at the kitchen sink.

"Everything was delicious, Poppy. I owe you so much."

"You absolutely do not. This was the perfect opportunity to try out some recipes for the appetizer section of my cookbook. I'd say the Yorkshires were particularly successful, wouldn't you?"

"Everything was successful." Kelly picked up a tea towel and started to dry.

"Not just the food," Poppy said. "That was a

beautiful service, Kelly. I'm feeling so much better about this marriage, now that I've seen you two together. It truly was meant to be.''

''Oh...'' Kelly closed her eyes. She couldn't cry. For once in her life she was wearing mascara, and it would smear.

''What's wrong?'' Poppy turned from the soapy water. ''How did I upset you?''

''You haven't upset me. My own jumbled emotions are so confusing...'' Kelly found she wanted, needed, to explain. ''I thought I understood what this marriage was all about, but standing up there with Mick I realized that I'm—I'm *crazy* about him, Poppy. Absolutely crazy.''

''Oh, honey.'' Poppy started to laugh. ''This is a problem?''

''But he doesn't feel that way about me! This wasn't to be that sort of marriage.''

''I see.''
And she really did seem to. Slowly the smile faded, and Poppy's forehead creased.

''Maybe Mick's feelings about you will change, too.''

''I don't see how they could.'' Kelly knew there was no need to explain further. Mick had given her the perfect, the only, chance for her to atone for what she'd done to his family. Hoping that he'd fall in love with her—the woman who'd shot his brother—was way beyond what she had any right to expect.

AND MAYBE SHE WASN'T in love, anyway, Kelly reasoned with herself later. So much had happened, so quickly, it was impossible to trust her emotions. Still, when Mick came into the living room after tucking Billy and Amanda into bed, there was no denying the pounding of her heart.

It was that of a woman reacting to a man. A woman wanting a man. A woman on pins and needles, wondering if the man wanted the woman.

But Mick obviously had a different view of reality. He sank onto the sofa opposite her, as drained as Holly's helium balloons, which were now sagging in pools of color on the carpet.

"That went well," Mick said, easing off his dress shoes and propping up his feet.

Did he mean putting the kids to bed, or the wedding?

"Now we can concentrate on Billy and Amanda." She knew she sounded as if their wedding had been just one item on a long to-do list. She couldn't help it. To talk about what the day had really meant to her would reveal too much.

"I was thinking of taking Billy for a visit to the kindergarten on Friday," she continued, "then letting him start full-time on Monday."

Mick was almost prone, his eyes closed. "Mmm, sounds good."

The urge to snuggle in beside him was so strong she had to invent another activity. "I should really dispose of these balloons. Billy and Amanda will be sad to see them all shriveled in the morning." She went to the kitchen for a pair of scissors, then began snipping off the ends of the balloons, balling up the spent rubber for the garbage.

"Where do you get your energy? I'm so exhausted...."

"Then, maybe you should go to bed." The remark came out sounding snappish, and Kelly wished she'd held her tongue.

"It's our wedding night. I thought we should mark it in some special way."

He was sitting up now, eyes open. Kelly wondered if her desire was a visible thing. She'd kept her wedding outfit on, irrationally dreaming of *him* removing each item, uncloaking the woman he'd taken as his bride.

Mick moved to the entertainment unit against the far wall. After a brief search through his CD collection, he made a choice and started the music—a love ballad.

"How about a dance?"

He held out his hand. Without a word, she set down the scissors and joined him. The music poured over her, like a river rushing through the narrow passage of a canyon.

She'd dated other guys in her past. The most serious of those relationships had ended when she'd chosen to transfer to Canmore. To her recollection, though, she'd never felt as she did stepping into Mick's arms. Their bodies fit together perfectly. Mick felt warm and solid and totally male. Her head naturally found the support of his shoulder. His arms seemed to instinctively pull her lower body next to his, while he tucked her hand against his chest.

The dance was perhaps the sweetest moment of the day. When it was over, she opened her eyes reluctantly, afraid that the magic would end too soon. She turned out to be right.

Maybe because he interpreted her fear incorrectly, or because he himself wasn't ready, Mick gave her the softest possible kiss good-night.

"No need to rush things," he said. "With luck we've got forty or fifty years ahead of us."

Kelly didn't care about those hypothetical years. It was right now that concerned her, and she wanted back in the fold of Mick's arms.

But he'd already let her go.

"Do you have everything you need?" he asked. At her nod, he seemed satisfied. "Go ahead and use the bathroom first. I'll check on the kids."

In the vanity mirror, Kelly stared at her slightly flushed reflection. What Mick had said was true. She did look lovely. Better, perhaps, than she'd ever looked in her life. Still, the unfortunate truth was that she herself would be taking off her bridal clothes tonight. The groom, apparently, needed a little more breathing room.

CHAPTER EIGHT

KELLY AND BILLY arrived at the kindergarten classroom half an hour before the bell on Friday morning. They'd left Amanda with Poppy at the B and B. Three-year-olds could be pretty distracting, and Kelly felt that this moment, this day, ought to be Billy's alone.

Abby Stevens, in a denim jumper and pink top, blond hair held back with a turquoise band, appeared much younger than Kelly knew her to be. She smiled warmly at her new pupil, but the gaze that skimmed over Kelly held a measure of reserve.

"Here's a hook for your hat and jacket, Billy. Later I'll take your picture, then we'll paste it on a teddy bear and hang it right under your name so it'll be easy to remember."

Billy, always the solemn child, was especially grave today. He removed his outdoor clothing deliberately, then hung the jacket and cap with precision on the hook.

"I know my name," he informed his teacher. "I don't need a picture to remember."

"Good for you, Billy."

"I can read other stuff, too." There was no trace of pride in the child's words. He was merely stating a fact that he thought his teacher should be aware of.

"That's amazing."

Kelly met Abby's questioning gaze with a shrug. She had no idea where or how he'd learned. It didn't seem likely that either of his parents had taken the time to read to their children. Not a single book was among the boxes of belongings Mick had brought from Sharon's house.

Meanwhile, Billy had been taking in his surroundings. "Sure are a lot of toys here. Where do we do our work?"

"What kind of work do you think we do in kindergarten?" Abby asked him.

Billy looked taken aback, and a little disgusted. "Don't you know?"

Kelly covered her smile by turning quickly to examine the finger-painted self-portraits tacked to the wall above the coat hooks.

"Well, the thing is, Billy, in kindergarten we do a lot of our learning by playing."

"Yeah?" Billy was obviously skeptical of the concept.

"Sure. One station you might enjoy is our puzzle corner. Want to give it a try?"

"Puzzles?" He considered the idea only briefly.

"Uncle Mick gave me one. I already know how to do it."

"How about trying another one?"

"Why?"

Abby looked lost for a moment. "Because it's fun?"

That answer obviously didn't impress Billy.

"Because working on puzzles helps with spatial perception, Billy. That'll come in handy later with arithmetic and geometry."

"Oh. Okay."

Kelly wasn't too sure he even knew what arithmetic and geometry were, but they must have sounded important to him, because he went willingly to the designated table. Abby pulled out one of the more advanced puzzles.

"Give this a try, Billy. Call me if you need help." Turning to Kelly, she said, "There are some forms I need you to fill out."

Kelly followed. Abby's desk was a model of organized clutter. Colorful plastic trays and tubs held sheets of paper, pencils, forms and schedules.

Abby gathered what she needed quickly. "These have to be signed by Billy's guardian..."

Kelly understood the question behind her comment. "His mom, then. Billy and Amanda are staying with...Mick and me...for the time being, but I'm sure it'll be no problem to have Sharon sign these."

Abby didn't hide her curiosity. "So you *are* married, then? I heard some talk in the staff room...."

Kelly felt awkward, considering how recently Mick and Abby had dated. Mick had assured her he'd spoken to Abby, but she had no idea exactly what he'd said, or in what detail he'd explained their situation. Did Abby realize, or guess, that Mick had married her primarily to provide a caregiver for the children?

"I wasn't aware you two were involved," Abby continued. "Frankly, finding out your history made me feel better about the few dates I had with Mick recently—I'm sure he told you."

Kelly nodded.

"Well, Mick kept asking me out, but I could tell his heart wasn't in it. At the time I worried that something was wrong with me, but now I know he was still in love with you. I'm glad you two worked out your differences."

Kelly saw no advantage to disabusing Abby of her romantic view of the situation. "It was a tough time for both of us. But eventually we got our priorities straightened out."

"That's good. I'm glad for you, I really am." Abby placed a hand impulsively on Kelly's arm. "I hope you'll be happy."

"Thanks, Abby." So did she.

MICK CAME HOME EARLY from work that night, eager to hear all about Billy's first day at kindergarten.

Kelly had phoned him earlier, making him laugh with her description of Billy's disenchantment with school.

"So how did it go, Billy?"

With an air of embarrassment, the small boy displayed a craft he'd made. "I didn't learn much," he confessed. "I did a puzzle. We sang songs."

Mick scooped his nephew into his lap. "Billy, there's lots to learn in life, and it isn't all about books. But you are a good reader. I noticed you sounding out the words in one of the books Kelly took out from the library."

He glanced over to the kitchen counter. Kelly had sat little Amanda on a stool, and they were tearing lettuce for a salad.

"Amanda likes salad?" he heard Kelly ask.

Amanda said nothing, just kept tearing. Billy answered quickly on his sister's and his behalf. "No. We don't like salad."

"But have you ever tried salad with my special magical dressing?" Kelly teased.

"What's so magical about it?"

"Once you start eating it, you just can't stop. I made it for my niece once, and she ate every head of lettuce in the entire grocery store."

Billy laughed, recognizing the joke, but Amanda's eyes grew huge. Kelly gave her a hug. "Don't worry, love. There's an antidote. One drink of my special antimagic potion and you can stop eating the salad.''

"Antimagic potion." Billy tried the words out carefully. He didn't like mispronouncing anything. "What's that?"

"You'll have to wait for dinner to find out," Kelly said. "I'll give you a clue, though. It tastes a lot like milk...but it's pink!"

After that, of course, Billy couldn't wait to try the salad or the antimagic potion. Milk with a drop of red food coloring, Mick discovered later. And Amanda, who always followed her big brother's lead, was the same.

"You're great with the kids," he told Kelly later, once the youngsters had been bathed and read to and tucked into bed.

They were doing dishes together—Mick washing, Kelly drying and putting away. In the past two days Mick had discovered he really enjoyed sharing simple domestic tasks like this.

"I've had some practice with my niece, Holly. But not as much as I'd like. Cathleen and I have been after Maureen to move to Canmore for ages, especially since Rod's death."

Mick had heard about the mountaineering accident in South America last spring. A climbing friend of his had been included in the aborted expedition. He'd reported back with great contempt on Rod's foolish disregard for the advice from their guides.

"He died from altitude sickness, right?"

Kelly nodded. "Rod was always biting off more than he could chew. Too bad he never stopped to think about his wife and daughter."

"Maureen seems to be doing okay, now." He'd met her officially for the first time at their wedding. And found Kelly's eldest sister's gregarious, confident personality a little intimidating. If she was hurting inside, she was hiding it well.

"She doesn't pretend that her marriage with Rod was heaven-sent, but I do think she's worried about her daughter. Holly worshiped her father. She misses him dreadfully."

"Holly is the one who brought the balloons?" He was trying to get them all straight in his mind. Kelly's family wasn't that big, but they were close and very involved in one another's lives. Something else he'd discovered, to his great surprise, that he enjoyed being a part of.

Which made him think of one very important topic he and Kelly hadn't discussed before their marriage. Children. Right now Billy and Amanda were such a handful he couldn't imagine taking on more. But one day Kelly might want a child of her own.

He wouldn't mind if she did. Actually, he'd kind of like it. Of course, they were a long way from making decisions like that. And even farther from being able to implement them.

Implementation, of course, would involve sharing the same bed, making love. An eventuality they'd agreed to—but when? He'd been ready on their wedding night, but he'd promised not to rush things, and he meant to live up to that. Even though the waiting was making him crazy.

Not since his teenage years had sex preoccupied his thoughts like this. Any little thing—a glimpse of Kelly's legs from under her housecoat, the bare inch of flesh between her running pants and her T-shirt when she reached for the casserole dishes in the top kitchen cabinet—could set his libido thrumming.

He might have written off the reaction as a natural one for any man who suddenly found himself room-mates with an attractive woman. But he'd had his opportunities with Abby, too, and had never even been tempted.

Of course he'd had other girlfriends. Women he'd desired, slept with and enjoyed. But somehow none of those situations compared with this, either.

So many times in the past few days he'd been tempted to reach out to Kelly. Never more than on their wedding night, when they'd danced and she'd felt like a dream in his arms.

But he couldn't stand to turn her off by moving too quickly.

"Mick, you can let out the water. We're finished."

He blinked, realizing he'd been staring like a zombie out the back window. Groping with his fingers, he twisted the plug from the bottom of the sink, then dried his hands on a towel Kelly handed him.

"Worried about something?" she asked.

Yeah. You. He closed his eyes. If he couldn't see her lips, he couldn't yearn to kiss them. But he could still smell her—that botanical scent he'd learned came from her shampoo.

She'd propped the tall green bottle on the edge of the tub, next to his no-name brand. He'd also discovered a pretty pink razor—on the high shelf, well out of the children's reach.

All reminders that he was living with a woman now—and that she slept across the hall and one door down.

"Mick, tell me what's wrong."

Not on your life, baby! "I'm fine. Maybe tired. But how about you? It can't be easy looking after two busy children all day."

"It isn't easy, but I'm so happy, Mick. Amanda is such a doll. She follows me everywhere and loves to help, no matter what I'm doing. Billy is harder. He's reserving judgment on me, but that's only fair."

"He'll come round."

"I just wish he could lighten up a little. He's always so serious and anxious to succeed." Kelly leaned over the counter. He watched her trace the pattern in the Arborite, noticing the gleam of her new ring. Without thinking, or planning, he touched the shiny metal. The ring felt warm—from contact with her skin.

"How are you adjusting to *this?*"

"To the ring? Or the man?"

His heart felt as if it were trying to lunge from his chest. "The man."

Her expression reminded him of Billy. So serious.

"He's a good man," she said softly. "I think I'm lucky to have married him."

The doorbell rang, punctuating the moment. "Hold that thought," he told her, rushing to the front entrance to answer quickly before the kids woke up. He pulled out his wallet, expecting a canvasser.

But when the door swung in, it was Sharon he saw, standing in the pool of yellow light from the outdoor streetlamp.

"Miggie. I have ta see my kids..." She stepped forward, but not anticipating the rise, tripped.

Mick opened his arms to catch her. She reeked of alcohol; her hair was oily and uncombed. "Jesus, Sharon! Not again!"

"Billy! Amanda!" Her voice was hoarse, and probably not as loud as she had intended. He fought back an urge to cover her mouth with his hands and, instead, pulled her to the living room, where he almost forced her down on the sofa.

He noticed Kelly peeking from around the corner, obviously reluctant to aggravate Sharon further. But she was clearly concerned.

Coffee, he mouthed at her, before crouching in front of Sharon and taking her face in his hands. "Look at me, Sharon. You're totally pissed. You can't see the kids like this. Besides, they're sleeping."

Sharon started to cry. "My kids. I hafta see my kids."

God help him, he could remember the times that his mother had been like this. Drunk, she'd want to hold him and Danny close. Then she'd kiss their faces and tell them how much she loved them. But all the while he and Danny would be cringing, recoiling from her vicious breath and the sure knowledge that in a couple of hours she'd be swearing at them and throwing things and complaining that they were "no bloody good."

"Come tomorrow, when you're sober," he urged.

"You don't *want* me to see them!"

She flung a fist at his shoulder, but she was so weak he hardly felt it.

"You and that new bride of yours are stealing my kids for your own!"

He knew better than to argue with a drunk. But he did it, anyway. "Nothing would make me happier than seeing Billy and Amanda living with you again, Sharon. But I won't let you mess up their lives. You've got to stop drinking—"

"Stop drinking! You say that like it's so easy! You have no idea..."

She started sobbing again, slobbery choking cries that stretched the limits of his patience. He got up to get some tissues. In the kitchen, Kelly was pouring fresh coffee into a mug.

"Here—" She pressed the mug into his hands, her voice urgent. "Don't let her near them."

"I won't," he promised.

But in the few seconds it took him to return, Sharon had already left the room. He didn't know how she could have moved so fast when she could barely stand.

"Damn it, Sharon!" He set down the mug and rushed down the hall. He caught her bending over Billy.

"Billy. Mommy's here. You're coming home."

Billy's eyes were open, his expression as alert as if he'd been awake for hours. He started to get out of bed.

"No, Billy. You're staying here." Mick put an arm around Sharon's back. "You can come back tomorrow to see the kids," he said as calmly as he could.

Sharon twisted and pulled. Mick glanced back at Billy. "Your mother isn't feeling well. She'll be better tomorrow."

"No, no, no!" Sharon protested, but he continued to pull her out of the room, down the hall, back to the front door.

Sharon didn't seem to notice Kelly when they passed her.

"Check on Billy, please," he asked. "I'm going to drive Sharon home."

She nodded. "Drive carefully, Mick. And don't worry. I'll look after Billy."

It was a warm comment to take with him into the cold, dark night.

"MY MOM NEEDS ME."

Kelly sighed. Billy was not settling back to sleep; she couldn't even convince him to crawl under the covers. The room was still dark. Fortunately, Amanda hadn't stirred in the commotion.

"I've got to get dressed and go home," he said. He tried to scramble off the bed, but she caught him under the arms.

"Your uncle Mick is looking after your mommy right now. He can take good care of her."

Billy couldn't argue with the qualifications of his uncle. "But she needs *me*."

His determination broke her heart. He was such a young boy—little for his age, besides. To see him burdened with so much responsibility...not just for his mother, but his sister, too. No wonder he was always so serious.

How could Sharon do this to her son and daughter? She ignored her children and their needs, but when she was lonely and feeling sorry for herself, she wanted them to cuddle and love. Her motivations were so selfish and uncaring, Kelly wanted to scream.

"We shouldn't have left her. She's all by herself," Billy was muttering, but he'd stopped struggling to get off the bed.

Kelly stroked down his wild brown hair. Billy stopped talking; his mouth stretched out in a yawn.

"Shh," she murmured, continuing to caress his head. Despite his best intentions, fatigue had him drooping back to the pillow.

"It's okay, Billy. Your mommy's going to be okay. And so are you and Amanda."

Billy's eyes opened once more. "Mommy..." He tried to lift his head.

"It's okay, Billy," she repeated. "You need to go to sleep."

Finally, he gave in to slumber. Kelly eased off his bed, then moved to Amanda's. The three-year-old had her thumb in her mouth. She was wearing a pull-up diaper now, to protect her bedding from accidents. Kelly tried to check if it was wet, but in the dark it was hard to tell.

"Sleep tight, baby." She kissed the child's forehead, then left the room, door ajar. In the living room she bypassed Sharon's mug of cooling coffee and went straight to the window overlooking the street. Adjusting the blinds so she could see outside, she prepared herself for a long wait.

CHAPTER NINE

MICK ARRIVED HOME just before midnight. Kelly was asleep on the couch, hugging one of the cushions to her chest. Quietly, he hung his keys on the hook by the door, then removed his boots and jacket and carefully placed them in the closet.

He was used to coming home late to an empty house, not having to worry about how much noise he made. This was better. The house was just as still, but knowing there were three people sleeping here gave the place a whole different atmosphere.

Seeing the mug of coffee Kelly had prepared for Sharon, he took it to the kitchen, rinsed it and put it in the dishwasher. Then he threw out the filter from the coffee machine and rinsed the pot clean, too.

Back in the living room, he found Kelly still asleep. She looked cold, the way she was cuddling that pillow, and she had her legs drawn up as much as the narrow sofa would allow. Should he cover her and leave her for the night? Or wake her to go to her own bed?

For a long time he stood debating. Until he realized he wasn't trying to decide what to do but merely enjoying watching her.

My wife. He had to keep reminding himself—the situation was so bizarre. And yet so right. They'd been living together for two days now, but the transition had happened so seamlessly he felt it had been much longer.

As far as Billy and Amanda were concerned, he knew he'd made the right decision. Kelly was wonderful with them, and if not for her, he'd be going crazy right now. Sharon was out of control, and the demands of his job were as great as ever.

He knelt and brushed back her hair from her face. Her lashes fluttered but she didn't open her eyes. He ran a finger along the line of her cheek, to the corner of her mouth. Her lips were pink and full in sleep.

"Mick?" Her throaty voice made him wish he were lying beside her, in a bed.

"Hey, Kelly. Want me to cover you up? Or would you rather move to your room?"

She raised her head, yawned, then rubbed her eyes. "What time is it?"

"Just about midnight." He claimed a corner of the sofa as she shifted into a half-sitting position. "Sorry I took so long. I tried to sober her up a bit before she went to sleep."

"What was she doing here? I thought she'd gone to Banff."

"Apparently, her new boyfriend said something

or did something she didn't appreciate. She came back this afternoon and headed straight to the bar.''

That Sharon's first instinct hadn't been to see her kids spoke volumes to Mick.

"Poor Billy and Amanda."

Kelly's sadness made Mick feel guilty. He kept forgetting that she held herself accountable for all this—Sharon's drinking, its effect on Billy and Amanda, and the potential impact on the unborn child.

"At least they have us," he said. "A stable home base for whenever it's needed.''

"I wish we could keep them always, Mick," she confessed. "And I hate to say this, but I wish Sharon would just leave them alone. Poor Billy was so torn apart inside after she left. He feels responsible for his mother, for her happiness.... Their relationship is totally twisted—not the natural roles of mother and child.''

He nodded, understanding, more than Kelly possibly could, how a kid might feel that way about a parent. Oh, the hours he'd spent worrying about his mother...and trying to be good so that she would love and appreciate him.

Yet Danny hadn't felt the same compunction. He'd been wild and rebellious from a very early age. Mick wondered about Amanda. It was so hard to gauge the effects of the past few months on the three-year-old. Obviously she'd regressed—but were the changes only temporary?

"I've been wondering if we should take Amanda to a child psychologist," he admitted.

"Me, too. But my gut feeling is to give her a while to adjust to living with us before exposing her to the process."

"That sounds good." Mick followed Kelly's yawn with one of his own. "It'll be morning before we know it. Ready for bed?"

The intimate question hung in the air between them for a few seconds, before she nodded and stood. He fluffed the cushions back into place, allowing her time to get to the washroom ahead of him. Once he heard the sound of running water, he went to check on the kids.

Both were sleeping peacefully. His heart filled to overflowing as he watched them. Whatever struggles lay ahead, keeping them safe and happy would be the ultimate reward.

"Beautiful, aren't they." Kelly was right behind him. He could smell mint toothpaste on her breath, and shifted to the other side of the doorway to make room for her.

"I never knew it was possible to love this much," he confessed.

"It almost hurts, doesn't it?"

He looked away from the children, to the woman

he had married. "Yes," he agreed. "It almost hurts."

BILLY SETTLED reluctantly into the routine of kindergarten. It wasn't that he minded going to school. He remained suspicious of the notion that having fun was not only okay but an expected, vital component of the experience.

Kelly volunteered to help in the classroom every Tuesday, while Poppy took care of Amanda. She could tell Billy enjoyed having her come to school with him, although he would never admit it. She got a kick out of watching the little boy interact with his teacher. Regardless of what she asked Billy to do, he could be counted on to enquire, "But what are we *learning*, Miss Stevens?"

And no matter what the activity—whether singing, crafts or sharing stories—Abby was becoming adept at providing the answer. Even now, with Christmas approaching, Billy's intensity didn't ease. He attacked decorating his gingerbread house with all the concentration of a budding engineer.

Kelly used the other afternoons when Billy was in school to do her Christmas shopping. She popped Amanda in her stroller—where the child often fell asleep—and spent happy hours prowling the shops on Main Street, searching for the perfect treasures to mark this first Christmas of her new, patchwork family.

One Wednesday afternoon, just over two weeks before Christmas, Springer asked her to meet him for coffee.

The staff sergeant was in uniform, sitting at a table, when Kelly pushed the stroller in the main door of the café. She wheeled carefully among the tables and chairs until she reached the window seat.

"Can I leave Amanda here while I get a bagel? She's sleeping."

Springer nodded. "I would've ordered for you but wasn't sure what you'd like."

"No problem." She joined the lineup at the counter and got a pot of tea and a sun-dried–tomato bagel. Back at the table, she waited for Springer to start the conversation. She assumed he wanted to speak about the Mizzoni case and the investigation into her behavior on that day, but, oddly, she didn't feel nervous.

She was confident that she'd acted in accordance with RCMP procedure. Even if, however, the investigators had found something she'd done wrong, she couldn't see it increasing the burden of responsibility she already carried with her every day.

"So how's married life?" Springer asked, easing into conversation with the skill of a seasoned investigator.

"It's fine. The kids are keeping me busy, that's for sure." Which was, perhaps, the major blessing of the marriage to date. Since the shooting, there'd been too many hours available in each day, compared with the activities she had to use them up with. But not any longer. Kelly was amazed at the effort it took to keep up with Billy and Amanda. She and Mick shared the cooking and the laundry, and a woman came in to do cleaning once a week. Even so, she rarely had an hour to herself.

"That's good. I've always liked Mick. He writes a pretty decent editorial most of the time."

"So glad you approve."

"I guess you don't much care, do you. I have to admit, I worried some when I heard you were marrying Danny's brother."

Kelly said nothing. She'd known people would speculate about this marriage, but felt no obligation to explain her actions to anyone, not even her commanding officer.

"Some people say you and Mick were an item before the shooting. Others say you married just to provide a home for those kids."

Kelly lifted the lid on her teapot and withdrew the infused bag. With steady hands, she poured herself a cup of the golden liquid, then added a dash of milk.

Springer sighed. "Still seeing that therapist in Calgary?"

Scott Martin had been on a list of psychologists the RCMP recommended, and the department was paying his fees. On this point, Kelly had to be honest. "Not recently. Since the wedding I haven't had much time. Actually, I was probably just about finished, anyway."

Springer watched her sip tea as if he were searching for something criminal in the act. "We've heard the results from the attorney general's office. As we expected, no criminal charges are going to be laid."

Well, that was a relief. Still, there were the internal police and the provincial fatality inquiries to get through. Kelly felt no impatience with the drawn-out proceedings. Although she hadn't informed Springer of her decision, she was still quite certain she wouldn't be returning to work at the detachment.

Unexpectedly, Springer reached across the table to pat her hand. The gesture of comfort caught her completely by surprise. He pushed his empty mug to the side of the table, then stood, revealing the black holster where he kept his gun. Kelly blinked, then shifted her gaze.

"Now, don't be a stranger," he said. "You'll feel different about everything in a few months."

She was left wondering what he'd meant. Was he talking about the shooting, her job?

Or her marriage?

AS HAPPY AS HE WAS with the tentative domestic pattern being established at home, Mick found his peace of mind being stretched thinner and thinner as Christmas neared. With the children becoming gradually happier, he had two main problems on his mind. One was Sharon.

Rather than spend time with her kids at Mick's house, Sharon preferred to take them to her little bungalow off Bow Valley Trail. She was always sober when she arrived, or he and Kelly would never have let her drive away with the children. But she wasn't always sober when they picked up the kids, and that was a real problem.

Word around town was that Sharon spent more and more time in Banff, and that the boyfriend she was having this on-again, off-again relationship with was definitely bad news. Despite the fact that her pregnancy was now showing, Sharon was spending no less time in the bars, and she still hadn't given up smoking.

Mick's second problem was his relationship with Kelly. How were they supposed to move past the "comfortable with each other" stage into something more intimate? Time and time again he'd let the opportunity to kiss her slip away. What if she viewed making love with him as a duty? He couldn't bear to have her that way.

Friday he came home, eager to *do* something about the situation, even if it was just talk to her. The house was abnormally quiet when he opened the front door. Yet Kelly's truck was parked out front.

"Anyone home?" Lights were on in the kitchen

but the room was deserted. He opened the door that led to the basement stairs and immediately heard music—raunchy rock-and-roll. The air was cooler down here and light glowed from a bare bulb in the center of the large, unfinished space.

There was Kelly, dressed in gym shorts and a sports tank top, lifting arm weights to the beat of Eric Clapton's "I Shot The Sheriff." He bent his head so it wouldn't hit the joist, then descended the final stairs to the concrete floor.

She still couldn't see him, and he wasn't above taking the opportunity to enjoy the long lines and taut muscles of her well-conditioned body. He knew she ran three mornings a week, getting up before he left for work, but he'd had no idea she'd set up a minigym in his basement.

The music ended, and in the momentary lull before the next tune began, he stepped forward to lower the volume. When he turned around, he cleared his throat to ask, "Where are the kids?"

"Oh, Mick. I didn't hear you come in..." She set down the two bar weights and placed her hands on her hips. The skin around her collarbone and on her face sparkled with moisture. But rather than look pleased with her workout, she appeared worried.

"Sharon came to pick them up around four. She planned an outing to Banff for hamburgers and then to a movie. There's a Christmas special showing at the Lux."

He cursed, not liking the sound of any of it. The weather was clear right now, so driving shouldn't be a problem. As long as Sharon stayed away from alcohol.

"Are they coming home tonight?"

"Sharon thought they might spend the night with her sister."

Mick covered his face with his hands.

"I know how you feel. I didn't want to let them go. But what could I do? She's their mother."

He remembered the call he'd ignored on his cell phone during the afternoon staff meeting. He'd forgotten to check later for a message. "You phoned me at work?"

"Yes, but…"

"God, I'm sorry I didn't call you back, Kelly. We were setting our holiday schedule and I was totally distracted."

She picked up a small white towel and wiped down her face and arms. "That's okay. What could you have done?"

"Legally, nothing. But I might have been able to persuade her to let me drive them, or…" Or what? He didn't know. Truth was, dealing with Sharon was making him crazy.

"Maybe we should phone Child Welfare," he said.

"Do you think?" He could tell she'd had the same idea.

"I was hoping we could resolve the situation on our own..." He hated putting his family's future in the hands of strangers.

"So far we've been doing pretty well."

"Have we?" He wondered if the underlying current of uncertainty was something that affected only him. No, he could see in the way Kelly didn't quite meet his eyes that she felt it, too. She was just trying to make him feel better.

"It's cold down here when you stop moving," she said. A white sweatshirt lay in a puddle by the portable CD player. With regret, he watched her pull it over her head. The style was long and sloppy, concealing all he'd been admiring short minutes ago.

"Maybe we should take advantage of the evening alone and go out for dinner." The suggestion hadn't been premeditated, but once he'd made it, he realized this was the perfect answer to his problem with Kelly.

What they needed was time together without the kids. It was so obvious, now that he thought about it.

"That sounds nice, Mick. I'll jump in the shower."

"Don't rush. I'll phone for a reservation, to make sure we get a table." Friday evening in Canmore the local restaurants were quite busy, thanks to weekenders from Calgary and holidaying skiers.

Lots of early snow meant most of the cross-country trails were open. And the big ski hills at Sunshine and Lake Louise were doing record business.

After his phone call, Mick prowled the main floor, picking up stray toys and board books. The sound of the hair dryer from behind the bathroom door warned him that Kelly would be ready soon. He'd learned that drying her hair was usually the last step in her grooming procedure.

He went to the hall to get his jacket and keys, and was standing there waiting when Kelly came out, fresh and beautiful and more tempting than any restaurant meal could ever be.

She was wearing a black turtleneck sweater and caramel-colored trousers, the color of her hair. She didn't usually wear makeup, but he was quite sure she'd put on lipstick tonight. And all he wanted to do was kiss it off.

"You okay, Mick?"

He must have been leering. Schooling his features, he opened the door. "Sure. Just hungry."

And not only for food.

God, he hoped he'd be able to behave without the children around as a buffer zone.

CHAPTER TEN

SINCLAIR'S WAS ONE of Kelly's favorite restaurants. Simple yet elegant, it was the perfect backdrop for quiet conversation—something she and Mick were in desperate need of. They'd been living together for over a week now. In some respects she'd learned much about him. He was exceptionally neat, couldn't stomach eggs for breakfast and never missed the eleven o'clock news before going to bed.

She knew other things, too. When a three-year-old girl insisted on cutting her own meat, only to send her pork chop flying across the table, he was amused, not angry. He could sit in an armchair for an hour, watching the birds feed on the mountain ash outside the window, and not consider that he'd wasted his time. Reading out loud was a pleasure, and his favorite children's book was *Charlotte's Web*.

But for everything she'd learned about him, a dozen questions needed answers. Tonight she hoped to fill in some of the blanks.

During dinner they chatted about work, about

how he'd decided to become a journalist. Local chartered accountant Harvey Tomchuk had advised him on selecting a good school, given him summer jobs and helped him with his applications for student loans.

In turn she confessed that she'd spent her childhood pretending she was a private detective, and after completing two years of undergraduate math and sciences had decided to join the RCMP. She shared the highlights of her training in Regina, then the years she'd spent in northern Saskatchewan, putting in her dues until her request for a transfer back to Canmore was finally authorized.

It wasn't until after dinner, when they were back at Mick's house, sitting side by side on the sofa, that their conversation shifted to more personal matters.

Mick had made them coffee. They'd switched off all the house lights so they could watch the falling snowflakes glisten under the streetlamps outdoors. The dark felt cozy and safe with Mick so close. All she'd have to do was shift her knee a few inches, and they'd be touching.

It seemed to her that Mick's gaze had been heating up over the course of the evening. But she couldn't trust her judgment. The happiness she felt when she saw him walk into a room, or when he called her on the phone in the middle of the day, was all too telling. She recognized the emotion, even though she hadn't felt it—at least not this strongly—since she was a teenager, head-over-heels about her soccer coach.

That had been a young girl's crush. Coach Brant had been six years her senior and dating a woman who worked at the Royal Bank and whom he'd later married. She knew now that his smiles and words of encouragement had been innocent of the ulterior motives she'd ascribed to them.

But oh, how she'd dreamed of that man. And oh, how she'd played soccer for him—determined to be the best, the fastest, the most aggressive. And all for a word of approval as she ran off the field, a smile, a pat on the back.

Those wild, out-of-control feelings were normal for sixteen-year-olds. They had no business in the life of a twenty-seven-year-old woman who'd suddenly assumed responsibility for two children under the age of six. A woman who'd married a man for the most logical of reasons, yet was suffering from the most illogical emotional responses to his presence.

"You're quiet," Mick commented.

"I was just reminiscing about my school years. You probably don't remember, but I was just two grades behind you. Do you know how many girls had a crush on you in those days?"

Mick's expression was dismissive.

"No, seriously. Even my sister Cathleen."

"Miss Popularity? Now I know you're pulling my leg. We were on the yearbook committee together, and she was such a whirlwind she used to take my breath away."

Unbelievably, Kelly felt a dart of pain. The diagnosis was simple: she was jealous of her own sister. No one, she was certain, had ever found it difficult to suck in oxygen in Kelly's presence.

"You weren't the only one," she said calmly. "In those days our phone was always ringing and most often it was for Cathleen. Mom used to tease her that she ought to hand out application forms to her prospective boyfriends."

Mick laughed. "Well, I was never that. A prospective boyfriend, I mean."

"No?" He couldn't mean he'd been immune to Cathleen's charm. She thought of Cathleen's comment about Lord Byron. "If you'd asked her out, she would've said yes."

"No way."

"Why don't you believe me?"

"She had her pick of the guys."

"And why wouldn't you be it?"

Mick looked at her as if she were totally naive. "A guy like me? With a family like mine?"

The light from outside was faint, but she felt she had a clear read on his expression, which appeared sincere. It was hard to believe, though, that he could feel Cathleen—or any woman—would have been prejudiced against him because of his mother.

Kelly knew about Mrs. Mizzoni, of course. Her drinking and prostitution were common knowledge. As was the fact that the Mizzoni boys had had different, unknown, fathers.

"*My* father wasn't exactly an upstanding citizen," she said. "Deserting his family, not bothering to visit or write. No one blamed us for the kind of man he was."

"That's different," Mick said, and he truly seemed to believe it was. "Anyway, it doesn't matter. Cathleen was never my type and I'm sure I wasn't hers."

Only then did Kelly realize how tense she'd become. She relaxed back against the sofa. "Well, that's good. I know we decided to get married for...original reasons. But I still wouldn't be thrilled to find out you had a thing for my sister."

"Are you... Have you been sorry we got married?"

His question startled her so much she almost spilled her coffee. "Oh, absolutely not!" she exclaimed, as Mick leaned forward to steady her mug.

"It can't be easy. You've gone from living alone to adjusting to three people you hardly know."

"Mick, I love Billy and Amanda. And you're not

exactly a hard man to get along with.'' In some ways, he was too accommodating. She wished he would tell her what *he* wanted every now and then, instead of trying to please her and the kids all the time.

''Well, that's reassuring. But you've got to admit, there've been some uncomfortable moments.''

Kelly wasn't sure how to interpret that comment. Had he figured out the way she felt about him? Was he feeling pressured to carry their relationship further than he was comfortable with? She didn't dare ask those questions, of course. They were too revealing.

She had to say something, though. So she opted for the oblique. ''I guess a little adjustment phase is to be expected.''

''Definitely.'' He reached for her free hand and squeezed it tightly, not letting go. She hoped he wouldn't touch her wrist, where the fast staccato of her pulse would absolutely give her away.

''Kelly, you would tell me if I ever did or said something that made you uncomfortable?''

''Such as?''

Their knees were touching now, and it wasn't because *she* had moved. As Mick's face drew nearer, she thrilled at the intensity in his eyes.

''Such as, if I was about to kiss you and you weren't ready…''

Hearing those words was such a relief. "Oh, I'd be ready," she assured him in the second before their lips converged.

Fantasy rarely matched reality, and she'd dreamed about this moment enough to be disappointed by the actual event. But kissing Mick was like taking a nibble of chocolate cake. The taste was so rich and intoxicating she couldn't imagine ever having enough.

Mick was gentle, but not tentative. The kiss went on and on. They shifted positions so that she was practically in his lap. He never stopped caressing her, although his hands didn't stray beyond her face, her hair, her shoulders.

She sensed him holding back, so she did, too. Kissing Mick like this was almost as frustrating as not kissing him at all, but she couldn't stop any more than she could press forward.

Time passed. It must have. When Mick put his hands to her cheeks and leaned away a few inches, she glanced out the windows and noticed that the snow was at least an inch thicker on the roof of her truck. Yet it felt that only an instant had gone by.

"Are you okay?" Mick—courtly, gentlemanly Mick—was genuinely concerned.

"More than," she said.

"It's late. We should be getting to bed."

She knew he didn't mean *together*. The cake had

disappeared, nibble by nibble, but she was far from being satiated. Still, she wasn't completely disappointed by his decision to take things slowly. Necking on the couch might be a little adolescent considering their ages and the fact that they were married. Nevertheless, making love would bring emotional consequences she wasn't certain she was ready to handle.

"Mick?" She let herself stroke the side of his face one last time.

"Yeah?"

"Do you think the kids are okay? I hope Sharon didn't keep them up too late. And that she remembered to use Amanda's pull-ups when she put them to bed." *If* she'd bothered to put them to bed. *Oh, please, let her not have been drinking.*

"We'll go to Banff first thing in the morning to check on them," Mick promised. He kissed her square on the forehead, the way he always kissed the kids. "Try not to worry."

But it would be better to worry, Kelly decided as she had her turn in the bathroom, than to remember how she'd felt in Mick's arms. Her body was still vibrating with the need they'd stoked in each other.

Later, in her bed, the longing was even harder to ignore. Mick was across the hall, one door down. He wouldn't turn her away if she crawled into bed next to him.

Sleep, Kelly, sleep. She focused on the open window for a few moments. The snow was still falling. She tried to follow a single flake on its journey, but it was impossible. Eventually, it hurt just to keep her eyes open. She relaxed into her pillow and was almost asleep, when she remembered.

Danny will never see another snowflake fall from the heavens....

Her responsibility, her burden, was back. And, as usual, the heavy weight pressed down on her heart until consciousness faded.

"COME ON, Sharon. What's gonna happen to them?" asked the new man, named Brian.

Billy sat on the floor, next to the almost closed bedroom door. Light from the hall fell in a long, narrow line then traveled up the wall. By sticking out his arm, he divided the line in two.

He could hear his mom's new friend as clearly as if he were watching a show on TV. Billy didn't like him. Not his eyes, which reminded Billy of the hyenas in *The Lion King.* And not his carefully friendly voice, which was as fake as the sweetness they put in medicine to pretend it tasted good.

Most of all, Billy hated Brian's hands and the way they were always touching him: messing his hair, clasping him on the back, punching him in the arm. There was something very cold about those touches.

It was cold on the floor, too. Billy had given up on the bed. Mandy had stolen all the covers. Plus, she'd peed in her pajamas again. His mom had forgotten to use those special diapers that Kelly called "pull-ups" so Mandy wouldn't feel like a baby for using them.

"Well, one of the kids could get sick or the house could go up in flames or—I don't know. It just doesn't seem like a good idea." His mom was answering Brian's question.

"Don't be stupid. There isn't going to be any fire. The kids are sleeping, right? And they'll still be sleeping when you get home in a few hours. Nothing to worry about."

There were some noises, a few footsteps, a sound like clothing being rustled. His mother laughed. "Brian! I thought you wanted to go out."

"Can I help that your ass looks so good in those jeans?" More rustling. "Hey, what's this? Gaining a little weight?" There was a long quiet moment. "You're not *pregnant,* are you?"

"Don't be crazy." Gosh, his mom sounded mad. "I've had two kids, remember. You can't expect me to be as thin as a girl who's never had a baby."

"Hey, take it easy. I didn't mean anything by it. Just wanted to be sure... Come on, let's go get a beer. We can do a little dancing. I'll make it all up to you."

No talking for a moment, then his mother again. "Let me check on them."

Billy scurried back to bed. Yikes! There was the wet spot. He shifted to the very edge of the mattress. Mandy made a little mouse noise and turned onto her tummy.

The door opened, and the band of light grew fatter and fatter. His mother's shape was just a dark shadow in the middle of the golden glow. No sign of Brian.

"Billy?"

"Yeah?"

"Is Amanda sleeping?"

"Yes, but—"

"Mommy's going out. Okay, Billy? Not for long and not very far away."

He couldn't believe she would listen to that Brian. She'd never left them alone before. And it was night! "Is Aunt Carrie here?"

"No, but she'll probably be home real soon. You'll be okay. Just be a good boy for your momma and go back to sleep."

He wanted to be a good boy, but it was so dark, and already he could hear strange noises outside his window. It might be a bear. There were lots of them here in Banff National Park. Signs everywhere warned not to feed the wildlife. But some people did, and that made the bears so they weren't scared of people, and they might come right up to the house and break through the door—

"Don't go, Mommy."

"Oh, Billy. Mommy needs to have a little fun every now and then."

"Sharon!" It was Brian and he sounded annoyed.

"Hafta go, Billy. Be a good boy."

The door closed and the band of light narrowed again along the floor. Billy heard the back door open, then close. The house turned dead quiet.

Billy thought of Uncle Mick and Kelly. They wouldn't have left him and Mandy alone; he was sure about that. Even when Kelly just needed some milk from the store down the block, she always took them with her.

The last time they were there, he'd looked into the tall fridge with the clear glass door and asked her if there was any antimagic potion for sale. She'd smiled and told him no—that was one of her own specialties.

He'd smiled back because he'd figured out about Kelly. Her magic salad dressing and potions for the tub were just pretend, just for fun. Kelly might have been sent by his dad, but she was just a regular person. A very nice regular person.

But not as pretty as his mom, of course. When she wasn't sick.

Billy tried closing his eyes. Maybe he *could* sleep.

But almost immediately, he started hearing noises he was certain hadn't been there when his mom and Brian were home. A rattle here, a creak there...

Billy yanked the covers over his head.

NIGHTS WERE NEVER very easy, but Kelly found this one excruciating. Almost every hour she was pulled from sleep by her worries about the kids. The more she thought about it, the more convinced she became that she should have stopped Sharon from taking the children. Sharon was their mother; she ought to be the safest person in the world for them to be with, and yet she wasn't.

With each waking, the memory of Mick's kisses would come to her, too. She could still feel them, taste them. Her chin and lips burned.

Just after five a.m., Kelly was relieved to hear familiar sounds from the kitchen. Mick running water, starting the coffee machine. Her room was still dark—the sun wouldn't rise for hours—but while sliding back the curtains, she noticed the snow had stopped and the sky was clear. She slipped on a robe and went out to talk to Mick.

He had donned a pair of jeans, but his feet and chest were bare. Wasn't he cold? Mick had the furnace programmed several degrees cooler for the night, and the automatic timer had not yet turned on the furnace and brought the house to normal room

temperature. As she stepped onto the kitchen linoleum, Kelly felt the chill and curled her toes, wish-
ing for her slippers.

"Mick?"

Surprised, he glanced over at her, simultaneously
pushing his thick dark hair back from his face. He
looked rumpled and tired and very sexy.

She wanted to hug him. To wrap her arms around
his smooth, broad shoulders and settle her face
against the solid support of his chest. Instead, she
went to the cupboard beside him and selected a mug.

"Did I wake you?" he asked.

She shook her head. "No. I couldn't sleep. Mick,
I think we should—"

"I want to head out to—"

They'd spoken at the same time, but both realized
immediately that their objectives were the same. To
go to Banff and check on the children.

"We should've driven up there last night." Mick
sounded regretful. "They're probably okay, but just
to make sure."

"I feel the same way. Why don't I get out the
travel mugs and we can have our coffee in the car."

Mick eyed the time on the stove. "It's pretty
early."

"I know." The drive to Banff took half an hour
or less, which meant they'd get there before six.
Sharon and her sister wouldn't be impressed at being

awakened so early. And they'd be even angrier about being checked up on.

"You want to go anyway." Mick read her mind exactly.

"If the kids *are* in some kind of trouble, every minute we delay could make a difference."

CHAPTER ELEVEN

MICK'S CAR GRUMBLED a little when he started it. Leaving the engine to warm up, he brushed the snow from the roof and windows. The crystals were light and fluffy and flew away.

His hiking boots crunched as he slowly circled the vehicle. The sound echoed, magnified in the fresh white landscape. About four inches had fallen last night. He hoped Sharon *had* spent the night in Banff and had not opted to drive in white-out conditions.

The front door of his house slammed shut. He looked up to see Kelly balancing two travel mugs of coffee with one hand while locking the dead bolt with the other. After tossing the snow brush into the rear seat, he ran to help her.

She'd thrown on her dark-red fleece with a black down vest over it and tied her hair in a simple ponytail. One thing he'd learned in living with her— she was the kind of woman who could get ready in a hurry and not fuss with her hair or makeup.

''Thanks.'' He took one of the mugs, then offered

her his free arm. There hadn't been time to shovel off the sidewalk, and he didn't want her to slip.

She leaned into him slightly as they walked. "Isn't it beautiful out here?"

He scanned the familiar landscape. His neighbors' houses, the tall spruce trees—all scalloped in white snow. Under the faint glow from the streetlights, each snow crystal seemed to sparkle.

"Snow is good at hiding imperfections," he replied. Even the old beater, parked in his neighbor Walter's driveway for the past year, looked magical.

At the car, he opened the passenger door for Kelly. She slid into her seat and he walked around to the other side. The car was toasty warm now. He turned down the heater fan a couple of notches.

"I hope the highways have been cleared."

"Me, too." He felt cozy here in the front seat. He had the illusion that they were the only two awake in all of Canmore, maybe even the entire province of Alberta. He wished Kelly could slide closer to him. The bucket seats prevented any such thing, and he wouldn't have asked anyway, but he longed for the comfort of her body next to his.

Even if he hadn't been worried about the kids, he wouldn't have slept last night. Kelly in his bed was what he'd craved. *Soon, soon.* While logic told him it wouldn't be wise to rush their physical involvement, her responsiveness had assured him it wouldn't take too much longer.

"Did you sleep at all?" Kelly asked.

"Hardly." He already knew she hadn't. Kelly never slept well. Many nights, he heard her prowling the kitchen and living room. He'd never gotten up to talk to her, figuring she deserved her privacy.

The tires crushed through the drifts on the road. He headed in the opposite direction from the highway.

"Let's check to make sure they didn't drive home from Banff last night," he said.

No lights shone at the family's little bungalow, however, and the driveway lay bare. To be sure, Kelly jumped out to knock on the door and check in the window. She came back, bringing a rush of crisp, cold air with her.

"No one's home."

"To Banff, then." He swung the car around and headed for the Trans-Canada. Once on the twinned, double-lane highway, he was relieved to see that the snowplows had already been by. Although it was still too early for sunrise, a faint glow emanated from behind them in the east. The mountains now stood out as charcoal fortresses against the indigo sky.

They passed through the park gates, taking the far right lane meant for permit holders and vehicles just passing through. The speed limit dropped to ninety kilometers an hour. Mick hated to slow down, but he did so. A moment later, a bull elk confirmed his prudent obedience by appearing out of nowhere at the side of the road.

"Oh, look!" Kelly said.

He took his foot off the gas pedal and tapped on the brake. The elk raised his heavy antlered head for a moment, then resumed nuzzling the snow, searching for food.

They passed the elk, following the curve of the road around Cascade Mountain. Now the dark mound that was Tunnel Mountain, and the base of the city of Banff, became visible.

"I'm sure we'll find everyone safe in bed." However, Kelly leaned forward and gripped the dash with gloved hands, the gesture belying her calm words.

"Of course we will," he agreed, but he upped his speed a tad. Five minutes later, he took the first exit into Banff. They drove down the main road, past the condos and lodges and alpine-looking motels. Closer to downtown, a boulevard materialized, dividing the two directions of traffic. Now small shops dominated the sides of the road. Christmas decorations glowed prettily from gas-styled streetlights.

He turned left at a sign to the Banff Arts Center. Carrie lived in a basement apartment about four blocks off the main street. Sure enough, Sharon's car, covered in snow, sat parked at the curb. He slid in behind, suddenly wondering what they'd been worried about.

"Maybe we shouldn't wake them."

But Kelly was already out of the car, blazing a trail through the snow as she walked around to the back of the house.

Mick followed, the fresh air on his cheeks invigorating after the half hour in the car. He paused at the side door—obviously the entry for the basement apartment—while Kelly kept walking to the rear of the house.

"A light's on down there," she noted.

Mick went to check it out. Back here, the snow was even deeper, coming over the tops of his hiking boots and lodging uncomfortably around his ankles.

"Can you see anyone?" He knelt next to Kelly, in order to peer inside the small rectangular window.

Billy and Amanda lay slumped on a sofa, asleep in front of the television. The set blared so loudly that Mick could hear muffled voices, punctuated by bursts of canned laughter.

"How can they sleep in that racket?" Kelly asked.

Mick decided he'd knock on the door after all. He brushed the wet snow off his jeans and held out a hand to Kelly. Together, they trekked around to the side door. There was no doorbell, so Mick removed his glove and knocked.

After a few seconds he knocked again, then a third time. Finally, a light came on in an upstairs window. A middle-aged man, obviously fresh from his bed, came to the door.

"What the hell's going on? Do you know what time it is?"

"I'm sorry, sir." Kelly stepped in front of Mick, speaking in what he recognized as her police officer's tone. "But we're worried about the children who're in the basement suite. Could you let us inside?"

"There aren't supposed to be any kids staying in this place. Just a woman lets it from me. Carrie's her name."

"Yeah, well, her sister and her kids are spending the night," Mick explained. "Come look in the back window if you want to see them for yourself."

"I thought it was kind of noisy." The man brushed a hand over his balding head. "Who did you say you were?"

"I'm the kids' uncle and this is…their aunt." He glanced at Kelly. Funny, he hadn't thought of her that way before, even though it *was* the reason they'd married.

"Well, I guess I could let you in. Just a second—I'll grab the key."

Mick and Kelly stepped into the small landing. On the left, three steps led to the upstairs, while to the right several steps descended to a closed door. Mick went down the stairs, tested the handle and found the door locked. For several minutes they waited. The noise from the television was even louder in here. Why would Sharon and Carrie have allowed the children to go to sleep that way?

The landlord finally appeared with a small ring of keys. Carefully, he singled out one and inserted it into the lock in the small brass doorknob.

"Go on in." He stepped aside so they could pass. "I'm headin' back to bed. Try to keep it quiet down here."

Mick stared at Kelly for one uncertain second before crossing the threshold. "Sharon? Carrie?"

No response. After removing his boots, he placed them neatly on a rubber mat by the door, next to Billy's and Amanda's Sorrels. No other footwear was on the mat.

He stepped into a makeshift kitchen, the kind you'd expect to find in the basement of what had once, undoubtedly, been a single-family dwelling. Right behind him, Kelly placed her hand on his shoulder.

"That television is *loud.*"

He nodded. Sharon and Carrie had to be dead drunk to sleep through the noise. His stomach felt as if it had folded in on itself. "Let's check the kids first."

They went to the back room, where the television was. Mick turned off the power to the set while Kelly bent over the children. Amanda clutched her stuffed turtle in her sleep, as Billy's arm rested protectively over his sister's shoulders.

"Poor Amanda's bottom is all wet...and look at her face—she's been crying, Mick. And even Billy—" Her voice choked up, and he rushed to investigate for himself.

Holding his nephew's face between his hands, he could see the tear tracks down his cheeks and the trail of clear, dried mucus from his nose. Rage almost blinded him as he remembered nights he and his brother had spent like this. Goddamit, why did some people have kids?

"This doesn't make sense," Kelly said. "Why were they watching television? And what made them cry?"

He wondered if she was aware how quickly her investigative persona had snapped into place. Worried as he felt about the kids—not to mention being mad as hell at Sharon—part of him was intrigued to see how Kelly cased out the room. She picked up an empty beer bottle resting on a stereo speaker, then held it up for him to see.

"Only one," she said. He immediately realized

the significance. Carrie and Sharon couldn't be drunk on one bottle of beer. The kitchen counters had been clear, so unless they'd hidden the other empties, which certainly wasn't in Sharon's character...

Kelly checked out the two bedroom doors. The first one she opened was clearly where the children had started out sleeping. Bedclothes on the double mattress were rumpled and strewn with toys. Moving into the room, Mick caught a familiar faint ammonia scent from the still-damp sheets.

At the next bedroom, Kelly knocked. When there was no answer, she pushed open the door as cautiously as if she expected to find a gunman on the other side.

But no one was there. The bed was still made up; obviously unslept in.

"I can't believe it, Mick. They're alone!"

As bad as it would have been to find Sharon passed out on the bed, this was far worse. Mick knew he'd been guilty of making excuses for Sharon at times. But no more.

"Where do you think she is?"

"Who knows." The bars were long closed. Perhaps she'd gone home with the new boyfriend. Mick looked at the door, itching to ram his fist into it. Kelly put her hand on his arm, restraining him.

"Oh, Mick. Can you imagine what those poor

babies went through? They must've been so frightened.''

He drew her close, and she wrapped her arms around him. To have her warmth, her substance, next to him helped.

He'd never been this angry. Since Billy was born, he'd done his best to help Sharon. Again and again he'd tried not to judge, just to be there, to assist when she asked.

But this was over the line. Leaving those children alone all night was a criminal act, and he could no longer ignore what needed to be done.

"Let's make some coffee and sit in the kitchen until the kids wake up," he suggested.

Kelly nodded but didn't move from his arms. After a few seconds, he saw her wipe her eyes, and he hugged her closer. The capable, proficient RCMP officer he'd known for so many years had a sensitivity he'd definitely underestimated.

No wonder she'd gone to pieces when she'd shot Danny.

"It's okay," he whispered now, running a hand over her head and down her ponytail. He lifted her face.

"The kids are okay, thank God. We won't let Sharon do something like this to them again.''

Tears made her blue eyes sparkle like a luminescent mountain lake. "How are we going to stop her?"

"After the kids wake up, we'll call the police. They'll put us in touch with Child Welfare."

"Oh my God. Mick, are you sure?"

"No. But I can't see that I have any other choice."

"HOW COULD YOU DO THIS to me, Mick?" Sharon shoved a kitchen chair against the table and cursed. Alone in the room with her, Mick righted the chair and remained silent.

Sharon was a wreck. She smelled of stale booze and cigarette smoke, her clothing was disheveled and her hair was a rat's nest.

She'd arrived home at nine-thirty that morning, to find a police officer and a social worker waiting for her, along with her brother-in-law and his new wife. Fortunately, the police officer had taken the matter firmly in hand, warning her that he wasn't pressing charges this time, but he most certainly would if it happened again.

After the conversation with the constable, the social worker had taken over. Clearly, this wasn't the first time Sharon had dealt with the social services department regarding her children. There'd been complaints from neighbors in the past—even prior to Danny's death.

Here Mick had reached for Kelly's hand. To know that not all the Mizzoni ills began with her was good for Kelly.

In the end, the brisk young male social worker suggested a solution similar to one Mick himself had proposed. If there were family members willing to take care of the children for a while, as there obviously were, Sharon should take the time to get her life back on track. The social worker suggested private counseling as well as following the AA program.

It was all stuff Mick felt he'd told Sharon a million times. Would it make any difference that this time she was hearing it from an outsider?

Sharon had appeared contrite in front of the police officer and the social worker. Once they left, however, she exploded.

"You're supposed to be family! Damn it, Mick, what would Danny say if he were here?"

What *would* Danny have said about his wife carousing with another man just three months after his funeral, and leaving their young children uncared for while she was at it? Mick wasn't cruel enough to ask the question. But he wasn't about to take any more flack from Sharon, either.

"You left those kids alone in this house, Sharon. Do you understand how dangerous and irresponsible that was? Do you even care?"

Sharon set her jaw and folded her arms over her chest. "They were sleeping when I left. I thought Carrie would be home before long...."

But her sister still hadn't shown up. God knows where she had spent the night.

"They were safe enough," Sharon insisted. "You're overreacting. You saw them. They're fine."

"They are *not* fine. Have you thought how frightened they must have been when they woke up and found themselves alone? They're only five and three!"

"Billy's a responsible kid."

"Responsible?" Realizing he was yelling, he toned down his voice so the kids, who were being bathed by Kelly in the bathroom, wouldn't be scared. "Just how responsible can a five-year-old be? What if one of them had gotten sick? Or decided they were hungry and turned on the stove. For heaven's sake, Sharon, there could've been a *fire*."

Sharon was backing away from him. "Almer was upstairs—"

"Almer didn't even know the kids were down here!" Mick became aware he'd been advancing on his sister-in-law. And that the urge to shake her was dangerously strong. He swung away and paced to the other side of the room.

She'd broken down; she was crying. Then her

legs sort of gave out from under her and she crumpled to the floor.

Mick tried, but he could not find one shred of compassion. "You take that counseling, Sharon. I hope to God it does some good. Because right now, you're a danger to your own children."

Between sobs, she cursed him.

"Fine. Think what you want of me. But know this. I love those kids and I mean to make sure they're safe. Even if I have to protect them from their own mother."

CHAPTER TWELVE

By EIGHT O'CLOCK on Sunday evening, Kelly was ready to declare Mick's house a state of emergency and call in the armed forces. The moments of intimacy she and Mick had enjoyed at the beginning of the weekend were long-forgotten indulgences. They hadn't shared a private conversation since bringing the children home from Banff. Toys were scattered everywhere—building blocks on the stairs, puzzle pieces on the floor, plastic action figures on the beds.

She'd wanted to make them a real, home-cooked meal that night, so in the afternoon while Mick was playing with the kids and attempting to distract Billy from the TV, she'd stuffed a chicken, baked a pie and prepared three different types of vegetables.

She'd so looked forward to sitting down to a family dinner. Also on her mind, she had to admit, was impressing Mick with how well she could cook when she wanted to.

But the meal had been a disaster. The only food Amanda and Billy ate without complaining was the mashed potatoes. Amanda hated the chicken, and

Billy refused carrots, broccoli or salad. The final straw was when they didn't like her apple pie.

To be insulted that the children hadn't appreciated her meal was ridiculous, but that was exactly how she felt. It helped, only marginally, that Mick had eaten *two* pieces of pie and claimed the pastry was the best he'd ever had.

Now Mick was tucking in the kids, and she still had a kitchen full of dirty dishes to contend with. Sighing, Kelly reached for the phone. She needed help.

"Maureen?"

"Is that you, Kelly? You sound wiped."

"I'm being quiet because Mick is trying to get Billy to fall asleep."

"So late?"

"Yeah, well, things have been kind of crazy since we got back from Banff." She'd called both sisters yesterday afternoon to tell them the latest.

"No doubt. Those poor kids have been through the mill. And you. I'm sure you don't want to hear this, but I really think you're pushing yourself too hard, too soon. You were in a fragile emotional state to begin with, and now..."

Kelly took the portable phone to the living room and leaned against the picture window. She should have realized phoning Maureen would court yet another lecture about how she was ruining her life.

She stared out the window at the quiet street and

imagined herself alone, in her basement suite, maybe watching television right now or reading a book, while Mick coped with his niece and nephew on his own.

Impossible.

"You aren't listening to anything I'm saying, are you," Maureen demanded.

"Not really," she confessed.

The loud, aggravated sigh from the other end of the line was familiar. "Fine. Some people pay me two hundred bucks an hour for my advice, but I suppose you know best."

"Maureen, I *was* calling for your opinion. How did you cope when Holly was small? Were there ever days when you felt that everything you'd said and done had been absolutely wrong?"

Maureen laughed. "Honey, welcome to parenthood. Let me tell you some of the disasters I've lived through...."

After fifteen minutes, Maureen had Kelly laughing again, her perspective returned.

"Bad days are inevitable," Maureen counseled finally. "But Billy and Amanda are going to be just fine. You and Mick are natural parents."

"Really?"

"Of course. Now, Kelly, would you promise to do just one thing for me?"

"What is it?"

"Go see Scott again. Just one more time. You

haven't had an appointment with him since you decided to marry Mick.''

Maureen's advice was like water torture, only more annoying. "There's no point. I hardly think about…about the shooting anymore." How could she, when the kids kept her so busy?

"Your problems haven't gone away just because you've flung yourself into the role of full-time wife and mother.''

Kelly rolled her eyes. "I'll consider it, okay? Hey, I really have to go. I have a zillion dishes to clean."

Mick joined her in the kitchen a few minutes later.

"I'm sorry." He stalwartly took in the mess. "This has been a hell of a weekend, hasn't it."

"Pretty much," she agreed. As she transferred leftovers into plastic containers for refrigeration, she wondered why she was bothering. If the kids wouldn't eat this stuff the first time around, what were the chances they'd want it warmed up the day after?

"I keep wondering how I could've coped without you." Mick went to the sink, turned on the hot water and added a generous squirt of dish soap.

"I'm guessing you wouldn't have bothered with apple pie."

"That was great pie. Definitely the highlight of my day."

"Oh, Mick. I don't mean to sulk. It's just every-

thing is so much *harder* than before.'' Before the
Banff fiasco, the children had been so well behaved.
Now they seemed to go from one disaster to another.
''I can't help worrying,'' she confessed. ''Are you
sure we did the right thing coercing Sharon to give
us temporary custody?''

Mick passed her the meat platter to dry. ''The
kids are confused, that's all. Being shuffled from
house to house, then the trauma of finding themselves alone when they were in Banff. I got Billy to
talk a bit about the experience. Turns out he was
scared to death a bear was going to break into the
house and eat them alive.''

''Poor sweetheart...''

''Calling in Child Welfare was really the only
thing we could do.''

''Are you sure?''

''If we hadn't, we'd have risked Max Strongman
interfering in the situation.''

''The mayor?'' Kelly was confused. ''Why would
he get involved?''

''He was Danny's father. Therefore he's Billy's
and Amanda's grandfather.''

''But does he spend time with them?''

''Not so far. And not ever, if I have anything to
say about it. I don't trust that man, Kelly. Never
have.''

''He's not exactly a favorite among the members

of my family, either.'' Especially Dylan and Cathleen, who practically him.

''I guess I can understand that.''

''But if Max doesn't want anything to do with Billy and Amanda, why would he get involved now?''

Mick had the roasting pan in the sink and was scrubbing with a pad of steel wool. ''He made a point of warning me that if I didn't get the situation under control, he would sue for custody. And not because he cares about the kids. Believe me, all Strongman's concerned with is his reputation. He won't have people in town thinking his grandkids are neglected.''

''That is so sick! I'd almost rather the kids stayed with Sharon than went to live with *him*.''

''Neither option is acceptable.''

She was beginning to recognize Mick's stubborn look, and he was wearing it now. ''Thankfully the kids have you, so we don't have to worry.''

''And they have *you*.'' Mick put down the dishrag and smiled at her.

With Mick so warm and appreciative, the aggravation from the busy weekend was easy to discount. Thinking over the past forty-eight hours, she realized that, except for the scene with Sharon at Banff, she hadn't seen the smallest hint of Mick loosing his cool.

''I'm not regretting my decision to be here,'' she

assured him. "It's no harder for me than it is for you. How do you stay calm when everything around you is so chaotic?"

"You're pretty calm, too."

"Are you kidding? I feel as if I just finished a month of working nights."

Mick laughed. "That's also a good description of my state of mind. But it doesn't show in the way you act. You're really patient with the kids, Kelly."

She was relieved by his assessment, although she couldn't quite believe it. One thing she knew for certain. On their worst day, she and Mick would be far, far kinder to the children than Max Strongman ever could be.

Thinking of Max reminded her of a question that had nagged at her since the Rose Strongman investigation had concluded. "How did Danny find out Max was his father?"

"My mother had a picture of Max, which she eventually gave to Danny. He was always nagging about his father, and I suppose she hoped it would shut him up."

"Did she tell Danny his name?"

"No. There was some kind of agreement. No doubt a lump sum of money was involved."

"So Danny traced him with just that one photo?"

"He wouldn't have been able to if Strongman hadn't moved back to Canmore. Then he ran for mayor and his picture was pasted all over the town."

"He would have been much older."

"Yeah. But Danny eventually figured it out. And Max gave him a job and enough dough to buy a nice set of wheels so he would keep quiet. I'm glad my brother finally got what he wanted."

"Did he? I wonder."

"What do you mean?"

"Well, he received a lot of money from Max. But maybe he'd have been happier if Max had claimed him as his son."

Mick shot her an odd look. "You're probably right."

The dishes were done. Now Mick set to work on the counters, while Kelly put the roasting pan back in the tall cupboard over the fridge. Seeing the kitchen slowly revert to order and cleanliness renewed her equilibrium.

"It's almost time for the news."

Mick was glancing at his watch, but she didn't want to end the conversation just yet. "Why were you never curious about *your* father, Mick?"

She could see the question put him on his guard. But he did give her what seemed an honest answer.

"I was acquainted with the kind of men my mother hung around with. I always figured I was better off not knowing."

KINDERGARTEN WAS WORSE than ever, now that Christmas was almost here. Today they were making

clay ornaments for Christmas presents. Most of the
kids planned to give them to their mother or father.
Billy didn't know what to do. He wasn't sure if he'd
be seeing his mother at Christmas. And part of him
wanted to give it to his uncle Mick, anyway. But
then, would Kelly's feelings be hurt? And what
about Mandy? He also had no present for his sister.

Billy squished the clay between his fingers. He
liked the way it felt but he didn't have any urge to
roll it out the way the teacher wanted him to.
Around him, the other boys and girls were using
cookie cutters to make tree shapes and stars. After
the shapes dried, they were going to paint them, but
Billy didn't want to do that, either.

The thing was, his stomach hurt. Like the time
he'd eaten almost a whole box of his favorite cereal.
Only, for days now the hurting hadn't stopped. Ever
since the police came and told his mommy she
couldn't have them anymore.

Now staying with Uncle Mick and Kelly wasn't
just a fun vacation. Somehow everything had
changed.

Billy checked for the teacher—she was helping
that blond Ashley with the rolling pin. Miss Stevens's head was bent over; she wouldn't see a thing.
He popped under the table.

It was neat down here. Kind of dark, but he could
still see everyone's knees and running shoes. Most
of the kids wore Velcro tabs, he noticed. There was

also lots of dropped clay on the carpet. That would make a mess.

Billy crawled to the middle, where there was more space, and lay down. It was sort of comfy. He'd like to sleep, but what if he had one of his nightmares, right here at school?

He wondered if his mother still had *her* bad dreams. The ones that had brought her to his room late at night, crying. Who would take care of her now that he was gone? Was she crying all by herself?

It wasn't right that his mom was on her own. He'd asked Uncle Mick last night why she couldn't come and live with him and Kelly, too. Uncle Mick said his mom probably wouldn't like that.

But it seemed to Billy that he should at least ask her.

"Okay, class. Time to put away your crafts." Miss Stevens's voice sounded kind of flat and heavy from down here. "Leave the ornaments on the table to dry, and make sure you put any leftover clay back in the containers."

Billy could hear the children hurrying to obey her. From under the table, he saw all the little legs and feet start scurrying around. Billy tried not to giggle. He was getting out of cleanup time!

"As soon as you've finished putting everything away," Miss Stevens continued, "I want you to line up at the door. We're going to the library, so make sure you bring any books that you're ready to return.''

More scurrying. Billy rested his cheek on his hand. The carpet smelled kind of funny. He wondered how long it would take for the teacher to miss him.

"Okay, let's go," she said. "Remember to walk, not run, and to be quiet!''

Billy kept his eyes closed until the room was silent, then he shoved his head up to peek around. No one in sight. He pulled the rest of his body out from under the table and wondered what to do. Opposite the door to the hallway was another door, which led out to a special playground area. Here the parents came for pickup.

Billy decided to take off that way. Kelly wouldn't be at school until the bell rang. So he could go wherever he wanted.

AMANDA FELL ASLEEP in her stroller on the walk to get Billy. Kelly was glad. The three-year-old had been miserable all afternoon. She'd cried when they dropped Billy off for school, refused an afternoon snack and thrown several puzzle pieces down the heating vent in her bedroom.

Now Kelly appreciated the opportunity for a little exercise and fresh air on this sunny winter afternoon. Recent snowfalls had settled comfortably into mounds in people's yards. Roads and sidewalks were clear, and that made it easy to push Amanda's stroller.

Kelly reached the school early and leaned into the stroller handle while she waited. She smiled at a few of the other mothers, and soon the tykes were spilling out the special kindergarten doors. With their boots and coats, hats and mitts, you could hardly tell which child was which.

Usually, Billy was one of the first out the door. Not today. Finally, it seemed everyone had left, and still there was no sign of him. Perhaps he was having trouble with the zipper on his coat....

She couldn't check because she didn't want to wake Amanda, so she asked one of the other mothers to do it for her.

The woman came back a few moments later. "Miss Stevens says Billy isn't in the classroom. Maybe you missed him when he came out."

"No way. I was here before the bell." Kelly scanned the schoolyard. Most of the parents had already taken their children home. Few were still around. Certainly no little boy, all on his own.

Past worrying about Amanda's nap, Kelly scooped the drowsy child into her arms and ran into the classroom. She found Abby stepping in from the hall, the principal in tow.

"Billy wasn't out there?" Abby asked her.

"No," Kelly said.

Little red apple earrings bobbed from Abby's ears

as she swiveled her head to check the classroom once more. Kelly noticed that the left earring had a little worm poking out from the apple.

"When did you last see Billy?" the principal asked the agitated kindergarten teacher.

"I don't remember. Maybe in the library… No, I don't think so." Abby's eyes widened. She rushed to a large table and inspected a bunch of clay blobs. "I can't find his ornament… Oh Lord, he may have been missing for a while."

"I've got to phone his uncle." Kelly shifted Amanda from her right shoulder to her left. Amazingly, the little girl still slept.

"We'll organize a thorough search of the school," the principal promised.

On the way to the administrative office, Kelly stopped at the hooks she remembered Abby showing Billy on his first day of kindergarten. His name was on the far hook, and above that was the promised picture. The hook itself was bare. Wherever he'd gone, Billy had taken his jacket and his boots.

"I doubt we'll find him inside," she told the principal, biting back her own panic. Billy was outside, on his own, but one thing her police training had taught her was to remain calm and levelheaded during an emergency.

She didn't think Billy had set out for home—she would have passed him on the sidewalk. So where else would he go? Perhaps to Mick's office downtown. Or he could have decided to visit his mother.

Assuming a stranger hadn't led him away...

Kelly knew that wasn't likely. Child abductions were extremely rare. Still, to think of a five-year-old out in the world alone was scary. And what would the people at Child Welfare think? That she was no better at caring for Billy than was Sharon!

"Dial nine to get out," the principal said, before heading to the intercom system to make an announcement about the missing boy.

Kelly sat on the desk and propped Amanda on her thigh. Her fingers shook as she punched in Mick's work number.

"Mick Mizzoni."

What a relief that he was in! "Mick, Billy seems to have run off from school. I came to pick him up and he wasn't in the classroom. His coat and boots are missing."

"What? That's impossible!"

She felt the same way. "I'm going home to get the car. He may be heading for Sharon's. Or he may have decided to walk to your office."

"I'll check," he assured her, "then drive to the bungalow. I'll meet you over there."

CHAPTER THIRTEEN

AMANDA WAS AWAKE in her car seat when Kelly arrived at Sharon's place. Kelly pulled up behind Mick's Explorer. Mick and Billy were outside, huddled by the side door of the house, talking.

Although she'd been pretty sure they'd find Billy here, seeing him safe and sound made her suddenly weepy. She opened the glove compartment to search for a tissue, then dialed the school on her cell phone to let the relieved principal know all was well.

"Amanda, here's a book." She passed over a lift-the-flaps board book that was one of the little girl's favorites. "I'm going to see if Billy wants to ride home with us."

Billy and Mick glanced over as her truck door slammed shut. Billy's jacket was unzipped, his hat in his hands. Oddly enough, Mick, beside him, with his rumpled sweater, unbuttoned denim jacket and disheveled hair, looked equally the part of the recalcitrant schoolboy.

What was it about those two? Something in their eyes, or was it the shape of their mouths?

No, it went beyond the physical, she realized.

More like an aura of...disillusionment? Sadness? Whatever it was, man and boy carried it like a shield against the world. And to think she'd once interpreted Mick's character as cool and detached. How wrong she'd been.

She longed to pull them into a tight embrace. Instead, she smiled. "You guys look a lot alike, you know that?"

"We do?" Billy's eyes brightened. Resembling his uncle was obviously something he didn't mind at all.

"How are you doing, Billy?" She squatted on one of the lower stairs to be at his eye level. Up close she could see that he'd been crying, although he was putting on a brave face.

Mick settled his gloved hand on her shoulder and gave her a squeeze. They shared relieved, yet anxious, smiles.

"I'm okay." Billy shrugged but wouldn't meet her eyes. "I'm sorry I ran off from school. Uncle Mick says I'm not supposed to do that again."

"A lot of people were very worried about you. Miss Stevens, the principal and, of course, your uncle Mick and me."

"I know." He sounded so sad, so hopeless, that Kelly couldn't do anything but hug him. Billy was stiff for a few seconds, but eventually his little arms came up around her neck.

"Were you missing your mother?" she asked gently.

"I was thinking she might be lonely."

Mick placed his other hand on Billy's head. Now the three of them were connected. As if physical touch could provide an emotional conduit, Kelly felt that Billy's sorrow passed through them all.

What a vicious cycle, she thought. First Mick had grown up without the love and care of his mother; now his nephew was enduring the same pain. Was it too late for the cycle to be broken?

"Maybe Mom could come and live with us."

"I wish she could, Billy." Mick's pain edged his words. "Your mother's sick and she needs help."

"But she loves us…"

"Of course she does," Kelly said quickly, stroking the face of the small boy.

"And she *needs* us."

"What *you* need matters, too, Billy. And your sister," Mick said.

"Amanda's waiting for you in the truck," Kelly added. "See? She's waving at you."

Billy gave a halfhearted return wave. "Okay. I guess we might as well go."

They were walking toward the truck, hands joined, with Billy in the middle, when Sharon's vehicle pulled up right behind Kelly's truck.

"Billy!" Sharon's joy was almost as distressing to behold as Billy's unhappiness had been. She stumbled on her high-heeled boots as she ran up the walk, arms outreached. But not, Kelly thought, because she'd been drinking. No, Sharon appeared cold sober as she engulfed her son in her arms.

"I've missed you, baby!"

Kelly turned to Mick, and he sheltered her with an arm around her shoulders. Did seeing mother and son clinging so desperately grind his insides, too? Kelly honestly didn't know what to hope for anymore. That Sharon would finally get her act together and provide her children with a secure, safe home?

Or that she would just disappear from their lives and let her and Mick have the kids?

"Where's Mandy?" Sharon asked, brushing the hair back from Billy's face.

"In the truck. I'll get her," Kelly said.

The little girl was watching pensively from the window. As far as Kelly could tell, Amanda wasn't as pleased as Billy to see her mother. But she cooperated when Kelly undid the car seat straps, and walked willingly toward her mother. Did Sharon demonstrate a little less enthusiasm in greeting her youngest? It was hard to tell. Certainly Amanda appeared eager to shrug out of the hug as soon as possible.

"Maybe the kids can come in for a while..." Sharon said to Mick. "I just finished my first therapy session. And I've been back to AA." Her face was desperately thin; her skin was pale and her hair clean, but without any shine or body.

Kelly felt for her struggles, for the efforts she was clearly making to turn her life around. Still, she agreed when Mick suggested Sharon come to their house, instead.

Billy, too, thought it was a good idea. "Maybe you could stay with us," he told his mother. "I'll sleep on the floor so you can have my bed."

It was a child's solution to a very complex problem. Sharon clearly didn't know what to say.

"Billy, that's a great offer. I'd love to be with you and Mandy again. But all of us living together won't work out."

"Why not?"

"Oh…" Sharon glanced from Mick, to Kelly, then back to Billy. "It's complicated, right? Grown-ups don't usually live together unless they're married, or part of the same family."

Billy frowned. "But aren't we all family?"

Sharon began to lose her temper. "I told you it was complicated. I don't *want* to live with your uncle Mick—*or his new wife*—okay?"

Billy shrank from her. Mick stepped up from behind to place his hands on Billy's shoulders. "You're welcome to come for dinner, Sharon."

She shook her head. "It's not the same."

Billy's eyes were so beseeching that Kelly didn't

know how Sharon could deny him. But she did. She opened her purse and dug for her house keys.

"I'll see you another time, Billy. Be a good boy, okay?"

There was nothing left to do but put the kids back in the truck. Billy sat in the middle and buckled his own seat belt, while Kelly refastened the straps on Amanda's car seat.

Behind her, she could hear Mick and Sharon talking.

"You're doing great, Sharon, but you're going to have to convince everyone—the social workers, and me and Kelly—that you've changed for good. We're not talking about a week of good behavior here."

"No sermons, please. I haven't had a drop since Banff. Haven't smoked, either."

"That's fantastic, Sharon. Keep it up."

LATER THAT NIGHT, after the kids were in bed, Kelly asked Mick, "Can Sharon do it? Stop drinking permanently and be a good mother to the kids?"

Mick considered. He'd been drawn, as he often was, to the view from the living room window, and Kelly had joined him, standing at the opposite end of the large glass pane. He shifted his mug of coffee to his left hand, then with the other adjusted the slats on the horizontal blinds. It was snowing again. The large wet flakes didn't seem to care when, if ever, they reached the ground.

"I don't know if it'll happen," he finally said. "But this world would be a pretty hopeless place if it wasn't at least possible."

"She didn't drink like this before Danny died...."

"Not in the past few years, no. But she and Danny were both recovered alcoholics. The pattern of turning to booze during difficult times was already established in her life."

"If she quit once, maybe she *can* do it again."

"Yeah, maybe." But the last time, she'd had the support of her husband. Now she was alone. Mick knew that without alcohol to deaden the pain, Sharon was going to have to face the reality of Danny's death and of raising two—soon to be three—children on her own. He wasn't sure the young woman was ready to accept any of that, and could only hope the therapy sessions were helping.

A good friend would help, too, but he'd tried to be that and it hadn't worked. He was fed up with Sharon. His loyalties now lay with the children. And with Kelly.

Every day the reality of his marriage sank deeper within him. He'd taken on a life partnership with this woman, and he knew now that while it had been in the guise of helping the children, it had also been about his wanting Kelly.

What else could it be? From a logical standpoint Abby had been the safer, the wiser choice. So why pick a woman who had shot his brother—a woman Sharon blamed and resented?

Because Kelly was the one who appealed to him. Because he respected and admired her. Desired her. He hadn't been honest with himself at the beginning. But he was now. And admitting his true feelings for Kelly changed his outlook on everything else, too.

Much as his family situation was tearing him apart these days, he knew it was so much worse for her because Kelly saw herself as the cause. Shooting Danny had begun a chain reaction of events that could have led to disaster for Billy and Amanda.

Did Kelly realize that she was in almost as much danger as the kids?

He'd taken advantage of her, marrying her as he'd done. Essentially, he'd exploited her guilt for his own benefit. Now his crazy life was hers, as well. He wondered if she felt that she'd been handed a life sentence in a maximum security prison.

"If she *did*, Mick...if she did get better and take the kids back, what would happen to us? We said we were in this for the long haul, but without the children..."

Mick stopped breathing for a moment. The question was valid, but one he didn't want to face. "It's going to take a long time for Sharon to convince me the children are safe with her."

"Admittedly. But if she does, what happens then?"

Maybe Kelly was unhappy with the deal they'd made and was searching for a loophole. Her expression was so earnest, almost desperate. That had to be it. He turned back to the view. "Without the children, I wouldn't hold you to your promise."

The words were hard to get out, but what else could he say? He couldn't add to her sense of obligation by confessing that he'd still want her. That he'd *always* want her.

She had changed everything. In her quiet, nondemanding way she'd added shape and texture to almost every facet of his life. Even if the kids had to go, he didn't want to lose her.

"That's what I thought."

She sounded not relieved but almost regretful. He examined her eyes for clues to how she'd wanted that question answered. Shadows from the blinds veiled her face in horizontal lines. Physically, as well as emotionally, she was only partially revealed to him.

Was it *possible* he'd interpreted her feelings incorrectly? That she, too, felt their being together might be special on its own?

He reached a hand to her cheek. Her soft, warm skin was only a temptation to move closer. She must have felt the same pull, because she met him halfway. Mick let his eyes fall closed as their lips met. The contact brought his aching desires alive with a jolt. *This was what he wanted. Dared he believe it was what they both wanted?*

Kelly's immediate responsiveness gave him confidence. She at least had to be attracted to him, to kiss this way. Every muscle and sinew of her body felt as though it were striving to meld with his.

"Kelly...Kelly..." Kisses just weren't enough. Not the last time, and certainly not now. He tasted her and pulled her next to him, this time letting his hands trace all her feminine curves and hollows.

Kelly's rigorous physical training was evident in her body. He felt the taut muscles in her arms and shoulders, down her buttocks and back. Sliding his hands under her sweatshirt, he caressed the curve of her waist—muscles here, too—then the swell of her rib cage.

He stopped exploring to kiss her again, then he checked her expression. Her eyes, rounded and slightly moist, willed him onward. So he grazed his hands up, skimming over her breasts, then returning to her waist.

"Let me make love to you," he said.

Kelly's answer was direct and honest, like the woman she was. "Take me to bed, Mick."

KELLY MOVED HER BELONGINGS into Mick's room the next day. One night together had made all the difference. Now she truly felt married, and happiness pumped through her veins just as surely as her type-AB blood cells.

"Could you leave work early on Wednesday?" she asked Mick at the breakfast table. She still couldn't believe they'd slept in the same bed, *shared* the bathroom this time. She'd seen him put on his plaid shirt and dark brown jeans for the office. And she knew, oh, how she knew, exactly what he looked like under the layers of clothing.

At Mick's raised eyebrows she added, "I was thinking we could leave the kids with Poppy and go Christmas shopping in Calgary."

She'd never had kids to plan a Christmas around, so she wanted it to be special. She'd already invited her sisters and Poppy for Christmas morning. Christmas Eve would be at the B and B. Kelly had no doubt Poppy had already begun cooking and baking for the event.

"Sure," he said. "We could do that."

Later in the day, when Kelly phoned Poppy, the elder woman was amenable to the idea. "Bring the children out here. We'll explore along the river and then bake Christmas cookies together."

Both children were keen, too. So after Kelly picked Billy up from kindergarten on Wednesday, she drove him and Amanda straight to the lodge. The kitchen smelled like a Christmas dream—all spices and sugar and fresh-risen yeast. Dylan was at work, but Cathleen and Poppy swarmed the children with hugs and kisses.

"My, Billy," Cathleen said. "Look at those jeans and that shirt. You could be a cowboy just like Dylan. Want to say hi to Cascade?"

"Sure do!"

So, apparently, did Amanda. She grabbed her brother's hand as if afraid he'd take off without her.

"You, too, Amanda. Don't worry." Cathleen laughed, then turned back to Kelly. "Have a good time at the malls. If that's possible."

Cathleen had always hated shopping, unless it was for clothes at her favorite western-wear shop in Calgary. Shopping wasn't something Kelly usually enjoyed, either, but today she was filled with anticipation.

Because I'll be with Mick. Alone, for hours. That in itself was a wonderful treat. The opportunity to spoil the kids a little for a change was a bonus.

The trio were almost out the door when suddenly Amanda balked. She let go of Billy's hand and ran to Kelly for a hug.

Kelly squeezed the little girl. For a moment it was hard to find her voice. "Bye, sweetie. I'll be back before your bedtime."

Billy had remained by the door, but Kelly went to give him a hug, as well. "Have fun, Billy. Uncle Mick and I will pick you up before eight o'clock."

He nodded, then surprised her with a kiss to her

forehead. The gesture was so like Mick that Kelly once again felt weepy. Blinking back tears, she forced herself to relinquish her hold on the children, then remained at the door until they'd disappeared into the stable.

"You must be doing a good job with them. They're attached to you already," Poppy said.

Kelly swiveled to face the older woman. Poppy was cutting into a circular fruit bread. "They're easy children to love." She snagged one of the fresh slices and wolfed it down in several bites.

"All children are," Poppy said. "But yes, those two are especially vulnerable. That wee Billy is always trying to act like such a man."

"I know. I wish he didn't take life so seriously. He doesn't seem to know the meaning of the words *fun* or *play*." She selected a second piece of the delicious baked bread, and ate it almost as rapidly as the first.

"I see your appetite has recovered."

"How could I resist, with your wonderful cooking?"

"I'm just glad to see you happy. And I doubt that the children alone are what's helped right the world for you." Poppy brushed bread crumbs off her hands, then loosened the white apron she always wore in the kitchen.

"You're right. And speaking of Mick, can I take a slice of this wonderful manna to him?"

Of course Poppy said yes, and five minutes later Kelly was in her truck, headed for Mick's office. It took an hour to drive to Calgary, and in order to return by eight, they'd have to restrict their shopping to two hours. But that ought to be enough time to buy the children their presents. She already knew what she wanted to get them: Amanda, a dollhouse, and Billy his first Lego set. Also racing sleds for both of them.

Back in Canmore, Kelly parked at a meter just as Mick came running out his office door. He pulled on his denim jacket as he moved, and smiled when he caught her eye. She leaned over to open the passenger door.

"Hey, Kelly." Mick hopped into his seat, then pressed a kiss to her mouth.

"Mmm." She put a hand behind his head to prolong the encounter. One kiss, just one kiss, and she could already feel her body reacting.

"Maybe we should just go home to bed." Mick pushed aside her blue cashmere scarf to nuzzle the side of her neck.

"Only six more shopping days till Christmas," she reminded him, holding out the slice of Poppy's bread. He ignored the food, instead burrowing his hands inside her unbuttoned suede coat, then sliding them up the sides of her silky smooth top.

"You look so pretty. I haven't seen any of these

clothes before. Still, nice as they are, you'd look even better without them.''

When he shifted his hand to cup her breast, she finally had to restrain him. ''Mick, it's broad daylight. Anyone could see in.'' As if to prove the point, Alderwoman Beth Gibson suddenly emerged from the pharmacy just two doors down.

Mick smoothed down Kelly's top and adjusted her coat. She put a hand on his arm and squeezed. ''Isn't that Max Strongman behind her?''

Mick shifted to improve his view. ''It is.''

Beth peered into the cab with narrowed eyes. Mick waved, then made a show of doing up his seat belt.

Beth did not wave back, but appeared slightly embarrassed at having been caught snooping. Beside her, Max Strongman was busy talking, oblivious to the visual exchange.

''I've seen the two of them together quite a bit lately,'' Mick said thoughtfully. ''Of course, they're both on town council, so maybe it's business.''

Kelly shifted the truck into Drive and headed for the main drag that led to the Trans-Canada Highway. ''I know Beth's husband quite well. Alan is a ranger with Parks Canada.''

Mick nodded. ''He's a good guy, but I'm not sure about Beth. She seems to vary her opinions to suit the prevailing winds.''

''Well, I certainly hope she hasn't made the mistake of getting involved with Max.''

''You mean romantically?''

''At one point Cathleen suspected them of having an affair.''

''You're kidding. Someone should warn Beth about that man. Doesn't she know he abused Rose?''

''Probably.'' But would it matter? In her line of work, Kelly had met many women who'd married a man thinking they could change him.

Mick settled back in his seat, stretching his legs as far as the space allowed. ''So where are we going?''

''There's a toy store in the little shopping center in Strathcona on the west side of the city. They carry the brand of dollhouse I want for Amanda. I believe they have lots of Lego, too.''

''What about the sleds?''

''We'll have to go to the big chain toy store at Market Mall for those.'' Kelly picked up speed to merge onto the highway heading east. At five minutes to four, the sun was now low behind her.

Mick pressed the knob for the radio, then set it to the local public broadcasting station. They listened to the hourly news, then Mick turned it off again.

In the sudden silence, Kelly realized she felt slightly uneasy, and tried to analyze the reasons for her reaction. She and Mick spent many hours together every day, but usually they were with the children, busy with their new roles as surrogate parents. It was only at night, in the comfort of darkness, that they became lovers, and that relationship was still so new—no wonder she felt a little awkward now.

Mick turned in his seat to face her. "I can't believe I lived in the same town as you for most of my life and barely knew you. I had no idea what I was missing."

"I feel the same way. Did you know that I used to wish you would ask me out?" They'd conducted many informal interviews for the *Canmore Leader* over a cup of coffee and a bagel. With hindsight, Kelly placed new significance on how much she'd enjoyed those encounters. "But you never showed the slightest interest in me beyond a sort of friendly respect."

"That's only because I'm a master at hiding my emotions. I wanted to ask you out, all right. But I had this policy..." Mick shifted his gaze back to the road. Kelly had the impression he was embarrassed.

"You only dated women from other places." He'd told her most of his past girlfriends were from Calgary. He'd never really explained why he'd felt he couldn't date the women from his hometown, but she knew him well enough now to guess. His childhood and his family's reputation were obviously sources of unhappiness for him.

"Why did you come back to Canmore after you finished studying journalism? I would've thought you'd be eager for a fresh beginning."

"I thought so, too. So I took a position in Ottawa for a few years. But I couldn't connect with the people there, or the landscape. I also tried a few other places. Vancouver, Kelowna. Only lasted a few months in each. For good or bad, I seem to be bound to Canmore."

"Same here. What do you think it is?"

"Well, for me a large part of the attraction is the mountains and the proximity to Banff National Park."

"Yes, but there are other mountain towns."

"Some people are more drawn to their hometowns than are others. In my case, I see it as a weakness. I won't feel successful until I've proved to every man, woman and child in Canmore that I'm not like my mother."

Or his brother. Kelly pressed her free hand to her temple. Mick rarely brought up Danny's name. Was it because he didn't wanted to stir her feelings of guilt?

"You've already proved that much," she told him.

"I'm not so sure."

Kelly stopped herself from arguing. Maybe there was one person who had yet to be convinced of Mick's worth.

Mick himself.

CHAPTER FOURTEEN

MICK FOUND IT TOUCHING the way Kelly was determined to make Christmas perfect for Billy and Amanda. No, not perfect. The children had been through too much this year for that. But if they had been exposed to an excess of tragedy, then it was only right that someone make an effort to balance the scales.

"Christmas is a time of magic," Kelly told the children. She brought out her own treasured copy of "The Night Before Christmas" and recited the favorite poem so often that by Christmas Eve Billy had it memorized.

Kelly drove the kids to the B and B where they made a gingerbread house with Poppy. She walked with them to the library for a Christmas video presentation. She taught them several carols and took them shopping for holiday outfits.

During the countdown to the special day, Mick was often assailed with bittersweet memories of his Yuletide holidays as a kid. Most of all he remembered the deep longing he'd felt for the traditions that he'd read about and heard other children speak of: houses crammed with family and food, candlelit Christmas Eve church services, cookies and milk left for Santa that were gone in the morning.

His mother had bought him and Danny gifts for Christmas, but the toys themselves had done little to ease his aching need for something deeper and more meaningful. Sitting in a pew on Christmas Eve, with Kelly and the kids and all of Kelly's family he was amazed that while he'd never considered himself religious, just being there made him feel more connected. To the world, his new family, to himself.

As the congregation rose to sing "Away in a Manager," he surreptitiously tapped Kelly's shoulder. When her gaze darted to his, he nodded to Amanda, standing between them in the pew. The little girl's mouth was wide-open. She was singing along with all her might.

Kelly pressed her lips together and reached for his hand, to squeeze his fingers with an emotion he understood completely. Amanda's voice was definitely off-key, but it was still the most beautiful sound in the entire church.

After the service, it was off to the B and B for a late dinner. Once again Mick was aware of the "magic" he'd always dreamed of where Christmas was concerned but had never experienced firsthand. He felt on par with Billy and Amanda as they stared at the splendor of the twelve-foot fir tree Dylan and Cathleen had decorated that morning.

The beautiful oak dining table had been laid in elegance, and when Poppy placed a perfectly roasted turkey at the head of the table for Dylan to carve, Mick thought his mouth had never watered for anything so much.

"Do you do this every Christmas?" Billy asked.

"Since I was a baby," Kelly assured him. "Not always in this house, of course. We grew up in a much smaller place. Sort of like, well, like where your mother lives."

Mentioning Sharon was always a bit of a gamble. Sometimes the kids became very upset. Other times they hardly seemed to notice. Fortunately, tonight there were many diversions.

"Did you hang your stockings yet?" Dylan asked.

Amanda nodded. Kelly had suggested they perform the ritual before church, as the kids would most likely fall asleep before they arrived back home later that night.

Once again Mick marveled at all the little touches a woman brought to a family. He thought of Sharon, then amended that thought. Not any woman. The *right* woman. He'd been so lucky to choose Kelly. She seemed to fill all the empty places in the children's hearts. And in his heart, too.

"It's time to say grace," Cathleen said. "Mick, would you do the honors?"

He was caught off guard by the invitation. To his recollection, he'd never said a prayer of any type in his life. He was aware of faces turning toward him, of Kelly pressing her palm into his.

"You don't have to," she whispered.

"That's okay. I'd be honored." Although he had nothing prepared, he had plenty to be thankful for. Looking across the table at his niece and nephew, he opened his mouth. And the words just flowed.

CHRISTMAS MORNING, Billy and Amanda were delighted with their presents from Santa Claus. They marveled over the missing cookies and the empty, milk-stained glass.

"I see some lip prints on the glass!" Billy said. He was holding it like a police detective, careful not to destroy any evidence. "Does Santa wear lipstick?"

Kelly laughed and her cheeks turned a little pink. Mick leaned over Amanda's dollhouse to whisper, "Next year, I guess I'd better drink the milk."

"Can we open the rest of the presents?" Billy asked. He'd been thrilled with his Lego set, but the big gift under the tree, with his name on it, beckoned. Now he looked at Kelly, the official setter of the Christmas rules.

"Not until all the family are here," Kelly said.

Both children accepted this as fair. Amanda hadn't stopped playing with her dollhouse for a second since she'd found it, anyway.

"You were right. Amanda loves it. It was the perfect gift." Mick came up behind Kelly and wrapped his arms around her waist. She was in her robe, still warm from bed, her hair tousled. Memories of making love next to the lit-up Christmas tree the previous night made him wish they'd been able to start the day in a similar fashion. But despite the kids' late night, they had awoken even earlier than usual.

No big surprise there.

Kelly turned so she was facing him. "Have you heard her speak? Since the Christmas carol, I mean?"

He shook his head. "Not yet. But I'm sure it's just a question of time."

"I hope so. I've noticed her diapers have been dry the past few nights. And she hasn't been sucking her thumb as much."

"I know." If only Billy were showing the same progress. But he still got ready for kindergarten each day with the joy of a soldier preparing for latrine duty. He seemed to live in equal parts anticipation and dread for his mother's daily telephone calls and weekly visits.

Sharon was coming this morning for Christmas brunch, along with Kelly's family. They were expected around nine, which was still an hour away.

"What do we need to do to get the meal organized?" he asked. Last night they'd made casseroles out of beaten eggs, bread cubes, cheese and ham. It had looked like slop, but Kelly assured him the combination would bake into a wonderful golden puff in the morning.

"Just put the casseroles in the oven and cut up fresh fruit. I can't do anything before my shower. Will you watch the kids?"

"Absolutely. Though, I'd rather come in the shower with you."

"Me, too," she murmured. Of course there was no hope of it happening. Mick made a note to put a joint shower on the activity list for the next time they had an overnight baby-sitter.

The Shannon clan were the first to arrive, at ten minutes before nine. First in the door was Maureen with twelve-year-old Holly.

Maureen slipped out of a very expensive coat and passed it to Mick. He laid the garment over his arm, noticing it smelled like her—some sort of sophisticated yet light perfume. So far, every time he'd seen her, Maureen had looked as put-together as a fashion model. When she spoke, however, she always sounded completely down-to-earth.

"Sorry to be a bit early," she said, "but Holly was so excited."

"Mo-om. *You* were the excited one."

"Oh, yeah." Maureen grinned, then reached into a cloth tote bag and brought out a bottle of champagne. "To have with our orange juice. Wait a minute. You don't drink, do you, Mick."

"Occasionally, I do." He'd toasted his wife on their wedding day. This Christmas promised to be another momentous day.

Next in were Cathleen and Dylan, with huge wrapped presents for the kids.

"Hey, Billy, Mandy. Did Santa come?" Dylan was in jeans and a western shirt. His concession to the holiday spirit was a pair of green socks with bells at the ankles that jingled when he walked.

"From my darling wife," he commented, winking at Mick.

"He sure did," Billy said. "Come and see! Come and see!"

Dylan stepped over the sheet of baking that Cathleen had set on the floor while she took off her boots. Mick finished with the coats, then picked up the sheet and carried it to Kelly in the kitchen.

Last in were Poppy O'Leary and a friend of hers, who also happened to be very familiar to Mick— Harvey Tomchuk, the man who'd once helped him turn his life around.

"How are you doing, Harvey?" Mick shook his hand and ushered him inside. The two of them usually got together about once a month for lunch, but somehow, since Danny's funeral, Mick had let that small routine slide. He'd heard, though, that Harvey and Poppy were seeing quite a bit of each other, and he was glad for his old friend.

"We have got coffee and orange juice. Now champagne, too. Which would you like?"

"Oh, coffee, please. How are you doing, Mick? Congratulations, by the way." He smiled at Kelly, then glanced at the children. "I see you two have your hands full."

Mick, as well, glanced at the kids. "They've had a pretty rough time."

"So I've heard. They're lucky they have you for an uncle, though." Harvey stepped into the kitchen and gave Kelly a kiss on the cheek. "And you for an aunt," he added. "Don't know why I never thought of you two as a couple. Seeing you together, it's obvious what a perfect fit you are."

Mick had to admit it felt pretty obvious to him, also.

Billy came galloping into the kitchen. "Can we open the presents yet? Everyone's here."

"Not everyone. We have to wait for your mother," Kelly reminded him. "And then there's brunch."

"Oh, yeah." Billy seemed to lose the excitement he'd had all morning. "I forgot."

On cue, the doorbell rang. It was Sharon. She'd taken pains to dress for the holidays, in clean black jeans and a pretty red sweater. The bulge from her pregnancy was clearly visible now, and Mick wondered when Sharon planned to tell Amanda and Billy about the new baby.

Sharon had two gift bags in her hands for the children, as well as a potted poinsettia for Kelly. Mick had given his sister-in-law some money last week to make sure she could get something for the kids.

"Thanks for inviting me." She was pale and still thin, but her hair held some sheen and her hands didn't shake as she accepted a glass of orange juice. Mick hadn't offered the champagne.

Brunch was a noisy yet fun experience. Mick could tell Sharon felt as unfamiliar with large family gatherings as he did. She sat quietly, her eyes darting back and forth. But she did eat a lot, and he was glad about that.

Over and over, his eyes were drawn to Kelly. She presided over the meal like a natural hostess, in her creamy sweater and matching wool slacks. "Winter white," she'd called the color while he'd watched her dress. The pearl earrings he'd bought her for Christmas had matched perfectly. He noticed that she kept putting her fingers up to touch them. Hopefully, that meant she was pleased.

"*NOW* CAN WE OPEN PRESENTS?" Billy asked.

"Finish your milk first," Kelly instructed. Across the table, she felt Sharon glower at her and worried that she'd been insensitive.

Billy, oblivious to the subtle power play going on between his mother and Kelly, gulped down his milk, then turned to Mick.

"*Now?*"

Dirty plates, crumbs and rumpled napkins littered the green linen cloth covering Mick's kitchen table—extended with a hobby table from the basement. A cranberry-hued puddle marked the place of the candle centerpiece Kelly had made with the children earlier that week.

"Yes, Billy," Mick said. "We can open the gifts now. Since you can read the names on the labels, you can be Santa and pass them out."

Sharon looked surprised. "You can read, Billy?"

"Sure." He seemed equally amazed that she didn't know this.

Kelly curled up on the floor by the fireplace as Billy handed out the first gift. Poppy and Harvey were side-by-side on the sofa. Cathleen was in Mick's favorite recliner, with Dylan on the floor next to her, his arm resting on her knee. Mick had brought in chairs from the kitchen for Sharon and Maureen. Holly sat with Amanda by the tree.

And Mick—he stood at the doorway to his office. Kelly was very aware that he was watching her with an expression that surely gave away to every adult in the room that something magical had happened in their relationship.

And something had. She brushed a finger over one of the pearls on her ears, remembering the moment he'd given them to her, right after they'd made love by the Christmas tree last night. They'd spread a quilt over the carpet, at about the spot where she sat right now. She wondered if that was what Mick was thinking about, if that was why he just couldn't seem to suppress the mischievous grin she'd so recently become acquainted with.

Billy handed out gifts judiciously. Well, of course he would take his role seriously. He started with Amanda, then found a gift for Holly. Kids taken care of, he moved on to the adults, searching until he'd found at least one present for everyone.

Kelly laughed when she opened the wrapped package from Maureen—a scandalous red teddy with high-cut legs and a see-through lace bodice. She laughed even harder when Cathleen unfolded a matching garment in navy blue.

"Mo-*ther!*" Holly groaned, rolling her eyes. "That is just so—so *tacky!*"

"Hey," Maureen said. "What better gift for my newlywed sisters?"

"Couldn't agree more," Dylan said, reaching over to slide his fingers along the fabric. "Mmm, soft. Nice choice, Moe. Can't wait for the fashion show later."

Cathleen slapped his hand away. "You be good, Dylan. There are *children* present."

"There may be *more* children present after we're finished...."

Kelly raised her eyes to Mick. He was laughing at Dylan's quip but looking at *her*. Picturing her in this lacy getup? Usually, she wore boxer shorts and tank tops to bed, but tonight she *would* try this little number.

The next round of gifts was passed out and the lingerie was forgotten. Billy and Amanda exclaimed over their sleds. Sharon had brought them action figures from their favorite cartoons. Maureen gave them books. Cathleen and Dylan had bought them each pint-size cowboy boots. Genuine leather, they were miniature replicas of the brown riding boots that Dylan and Cathleen favored.

For Billy, the boots were *it*. He yanked them on as soon as he'd unwrapped them, and Kelly suspected he'd be arguing to sleep in them later that night.

Seeing the children so happy and having the family together felt wonderful. The glow of Cathleen and Dylan's love, the growing attachment between Poppy and Harvey, even the new level of intimacy between her and Mick, added warm, tender notes to the atmosphere.

Kelly couldn't help but be aware, however, of a few darker undercurrents. Holly's animosity toward her mother, for one. No matter what Maureen said or did, Holly made sure to insert a quick, cutting comment. The lack of warmth between them was especially obvious when Holly unwrapped a leather jacket from her mother that must have cost a small fortune.

"That's nice. Thank you, Mother."

Like a slab of ice, the comment skidded across the room. It took a few beats before anyone spoke.

"I would've *killed* for a jacket like that when I was your age," Cathleen said, sounding envious. "And I've always thought that toasted almond color looks great on blondes. What else is under that tree, Billy?"

Next up was a gift for Sharon. She was another source of malcontent in the cozy gathering. Clearly, she felt uncomfortable with the new roles Mick and Kelly had in her children's lives. Now she unwrapped the denim slacks with an adjustable waistband, which Kelly had purchased at a special maternity shop in Calgary. She stared at the garment as if unsure what to make of it.

Kelly checked out Mick. He shrugged, and she felt better. She'd *tried* to select something Sharon would appreciate. "If you don't like them, or they don't fit," she told Sharon, "you can exchange them."

Sharon nodded, then finally said thanks, albeit a little curtly. She closed the lid on the box and shoved it under her chair.

The final gift under the tree was a tiny wrapped box no bigger than Amanda's hand. Billy stood in the center of the room, holding it like a piece of garbage, clearly distressed, cheeks flushed as he gazed at the pointed toes of his new boots.

"What's that, Billy?" Mick asked softly.

"I don't know," Billy said.

"Let me see." Mick held out his hand, and Billy dropped the small present like a hot potato. Mick turned it around. "No label."

"It's for you and Kelly," Billy said. "And for Amanda and…and Mommy, too."

"Is it from you, Billy?"

He nodded.

"Okay. Why don't we let your mommy open it, then."

"Sure." Billy was still apparently transfixed by his boots.

Mick passed the gift to Sharon, who unwrapped it cautiously. It was a clay Christmas ornament. A snowflake decorated with white glitter paint.

"I thought we could hang it on the tree," Billy said. He watched his mother's face anxiously now. "And it could, um, sort of just belong to everyone. Is that okay?"

The room went quiet as everyone waited for a reaction—even just a smile or a nod—from Sharon.

But the young woman didn't speak. She handed the box to Billy, her eyes suddenly red and watery.

"It's a beautiful ornament." Kelly rose to inspect it. "Billy, it's so delicate! Can Amanda hang it on the tree for us?"

What had gotten into Sharon? Couldn't she say *anything?* Billy would think she didn't like his gift!

Billy nodded, and Kelly gently passed the fragile ornament to Amanda. "Careful now, Mandy. Just loop this end around a branch—"

Abruptly, Sharon stood, then started for the door. Mick and Kelly exchanged a glance. *She was leaving? Now?* With a shrug, Mick picked up the maternity store box from under her chair and followed her. "Don't forget this."

"I've got to *go*" was all she said. She accepted the gift, stuffing it under her arm, then slipped out the door as if chased by fire.

For a moment everyone stayed quiet. Kelly wanted to say something to reassure Billy. She wanted to tell him that his mother had *really* liked his present. That she hadn't meant to leave without saying goodbye to her children. That she honestly did love them, more than anything else in the world.

But would she be telling him the truth if she said all that? Or just setting him up for more disappointment?

CHAPTER FIFTEEN

JANUARY PASSED so smoothly that Kelly began to fool herself into believing life was perfect. In three or four weeks she would have to start preparing for her testimony at the povincial fatality inquiry into Danny's death. But for now she could focus on family. Billy had begun to warm up to kindergarten. Amanda hardly ever wet the bed or sucked her thumb anymore. Schooldays settled into an easy routine, and Kelly enjoyed every moment with the kids. There was no question, however, that the highlight of each day was the time she spent with Mick after the little ones were tucked in.

They'd gone about their relationship totally backward. Getting married first, falling in love second. But they *were* falling in love, discovering each other in the sort of intimate, occasionally trite, way that all new couples tend to do.

"Do you *really* like liver and onions?" Kelly couldn't believe that Mick would order them for dinner, on one of their rare evenings without children at the local pub.

Then later, that same night, in bed... "You fantasize about Eric Clapton when you're working out?'' Mick asked. They'd just finished making love with ''Wonderful Tonight'' playing in the background.

''Do you have a problem with that?''

Mick wrapped an arm around her waist, pulling her, spoon fashion, into the curve of his body. ''No. Unless— Do you fantasize about him when we're—''

''No!''

For the entire month, Sharon kept such a low profile that Kelly could go days without thinking—or worrying—about her. She knew, via Mick, that Sharon still attended AA meetings as well as weekly sessions with a counselor. Given that the woman was sticking to the program, Kelly considered it strange she didn't spend more time with her kids. Billy and Amanda asked about her and phoned often, but that was the extent of their contact.

Kelly didn't go out of her way to change that. The young mother's behavior at Christmas was hard to get over. Like a petulant child, Sharon seemed to consider only her own feelings and wants, whatever the situation. Even if Sharon did manage to overcome her drinking problem, Kelly doubted that her fundamental character would ever change.

Which made Kelly dread the possibility that Billy and Amanda would eventually return to their mother. How could she hand the children over to a woman like that? Yet how could she not? Just as she had an obligation to the kids, she had a duty to Sharon, as well. Because Danny had been Sharon's husband and Kelly had taken him away, she couldn't take away her children, too.

The conundrum was easy to ignore, though, while Sharon was making herself scarce. The weeks slipped by, each one a gift that Kelly counted herself lucky to experience.

And then came the phone call from Bob Prescott, the social worker monitoring Sharon's case. Mick took the call at work, and Kelly didn't hear about it until later that night, after they'd made love.

"He wants us to meet at Sharon's place to talk over the future." Mick stared at the far wall. Flickering light from a candle on the bedside table created moving shadows over his face, alternately highlighting his well-defined cheekbones, his full, sensuous lips.

"That doesn't sound good," she said.

"No. It doesn't."

The next afternoon, after dropping Billy and Amanda off at the B and B, she and Mick drove to Sharon's bungalow.

"I'm scared," Kelly confessed as they pulled in behind a red, midsize car, presumably belonging to the social worker. It was a frigid winter day, so cold she could feel her skin tighten the second she stepped out of the car.

''So am I.'' Mick's gloved hand encircled hers as they went up the walk together. They stepped over the long orange electrical extension cord linking the house to the block heater of Sharon's old Buick.

Sharon opened the side door for them before they knocked. Her black leggings displayed legs still too thin, but beneath her hip-length sweatshirt, her stomach had rounded in the four weeks since Christmas.

The social worker, Bob Prescott, sat at the kitchen table, drinking coffee. An innocuous man in his midthirties, he wore a wedding ring and conventional clothing—and two studs in his left ear. One hand curved around a half-empty coffee cup; the other rested on a neat stack of papers on the table in front of him. Kelly felt a twinge of foreboding when he made only the briefest of eye contact with her and Mick.

Mick pulled up a chair for her, and Kelly sank into it. She wasn't interested in food or drink, but nodded anyway when Sharon offered her a mug of coffee.

''Thanks.''

Mick remained standing until Sharon was seated next to the social worker. Then he took the chair beside Kelly. They were squared off now, and the adversarial positions reminded Kelly of the many times she'd sat opposite a suspect to ask him questions. She wondered if any of them had ever felt as she did now. That sometimes the law wasn't great at producing justice. That sometimes there was nothing that could be done to protect the innocent.

"You are aware," the social worker said, cutting into the silence, "that Sharon has made remarkable strides since we agreed you two would take the children for a while."

Oh, no—oh, no—oh, no… Of course she'd expected this; she and Mick both had. She felt him press his hand over hers, but couldn't tell what message he was trying to give. Comfort? A warning? Probably she should sit quietly and listen. But she didn't want to hear what was coming next.

"Billy and Amanda are making remarkable strides, too," she said. "Billy's teacher tells me he's reading at a grade-two level, and Amanda's just learned her colors and she—"

"That's fine," Bob cut in. "I'm sure you and Mick are doing a wonderful job with them—"

"Like hell!" Sharon interjected. "They're trying to steal my children is what they're doing!"

Sharon's accusation wasn't unexpected, but it still hurt. Kelly lowered her gaze to the table, reminding herself that this woman had reason to be angry. Kelly had killed Danny. Now, in Sharon's mind at least, Kelly had stolen her children.

"You don't believe that," Mick said, pressing harder on Kelly's hand. "We just want Billy and Amanda to be healthy and happy."

"I saw you at Christmas! You've got them

wrapped around your little finger. Everything you say, they do. They've forgotten all about me! They're my babies. They should be with me!''

"Calm down, Sharon." Bob patted her back. "It's okay, it's okay...of course your children belong with you."

Mick squeezed Kelly's fingers. It sounded as though Bob Prescott had already made up his mind that Billy and Amanda should return to Sharon. But was the woman really ready? She still seemed far more concerned about herself than about the children.

Yet Sharon's suffering was so obvious, so raw, that Kelly couldn't remain unmoved. She leaned over the table in a sincere gesture. "Sharon, our goal was never to separate you from your children. Why haven't you spent more time with them? You know we would've done everything we could to cooperate."

"I can't stand to see them with *you*. Or with *him*. I want them home."

"But are you sure you can handle the day-to-day responsibility?" Mick asked. "You can spend as much time with them at our place as you want without having to worry about meals or laundry or any of that hassle."

Although his voice was low and calm, Kelly felt the tension in his hand and knew he was reining in a great deal of anger. Mick had never forgiven

Sharon for leaving her kids alone that night in Banff. His reaction said a great deal about his character. Mick was a patient man who would bend over backward to help someone in trouble. And he could put up with mistakes, was willing to give a second chance and a third.

But once you crossed the line with him, that was it. He washed his hands and didn't look back. And that morning in Banff, he'd washed his hands of Sharon. Now the prospect of relinquishing care of his brother's kids to this woman was obviously killing him.

"A mother shouldn't have to book an appointment to see her own kids!"

"Hang on, Sharon." Bob Prescott gave Mick and Kelly a stern look. "In my opinion Sharon has earned a second chance. This conversation isn't about debating that point. I merely wanted to consult with you on the best time and method of handing them over."

The man sounded as if he were speaking about a briefcase of unmarked bills, not two children! Kelly turned to Mick. He'd gone pale and very quiet. She didn't think he would be able to say anything, so she spoke, instead.

"Maybe we could do it this weekend, on Saturday? That way Billy will have a little time to settle before school on Monday."

"No, I can't wait—"

But Bob Prescott interrupted Sharon. "That's reasonable, Sharon. We have to think of the kids."

Yet, were they thinking of the kids? Each time they were shuffled from one house to the next they became more confused and their adjustment time took longer. Kelly wanted to cry at the prospect of telling them they would have to pack up again.

"Let's say ten in the morning," the social worker stated. "I'll be here to help with any transition problems." *Such as wacky aunts and uncles who decide to take matters into their own hands and abscond with the children....*

Kelly couldn't stop herself from grimacing. She and Mick stood. It seemed as if the floor had tilted to an odd angle while they'd been conversing. She stumbled a little; Mick steadied her.

"Goodbye, Bob, Sharon," she said, but Mick didn't utter a word as they walked out the door.

They were almost at the car when Mick stopped dead. Kelly tightened her hold on his hand, waiting.

"We could fight this," Mick said. "Let's go to Calgary and talk to your sister, see what options we have."

Kelly wasn't sure if he was serious or just venting. "A custody battle could get very ugly. You want to put the children through *that?*"

"I don't want to put them through living with *her,* either." Mick nodded back at the house. "I don't trust her judgment anymore."

"I know." She sucked in a breath of air, and felt as if she'd inhaled a hundred tiny icicles. They had to consider the kids' best interests, not their mother's. Billy and Amanda still loved their mother. Perhaps they would be happy under her full-time care.

Mick opened the car door for Kelly, then walked around to the driver's side and got in. He inserted the key in the ignition and gave it a twist. Although they'd been in the house for half an hour at most, the starter rumbled a little, protesting the thirty-below temperature and pervasive winds.

Kelly sat on the cold-stiffened leather seat. Her breath came out as tiny white clouds, which soon fogged the interior window. Mick turned on the defrost.

"I'm sorry, Mick."

"Why should *you* apologize?" He pounded the steering wheel. "I don't know how I'm going to face those kids."

He might not know how he was going to do it, but Kelly knew that he would. Just as she must, too. Neither of them could do anything else.

Except pray that somehow the kids would emerge from all this chaos unscathed.

IT HAPPENED AS PLANNED on Saturday morning at ten o'clock. Kelly felt as tense and worried as if she were delivering on a ransom request: *Okay, here are the kids. Now pass over a note promising you won't hurt them.*

The social worker's red car was on the street again, just behind Sharon's clunker, which was still plugged into the house with the orange extension cord.

Mick and Kelly had tried to prepare the children by emphasizing the positive as much as they could. No one was fooled, however. The children had slept restlessly these past few days, with Amanda once more wetting the bed and Billy reverting to his quiet, solemn self.

Kelly had packed their clothing and toys into two suitcases. "Why don't we leave a few books for when you come to visit," she suggested.

She hoped that they *would* come to visit, but the chances didn't seem good with Sharon so bitter toward her and Mick.

In the kitchen of the yellow bungalow, Sharon was baking chocolate chip cookies. The first batch was piled on the counter. Too flat, burned on the edges. Kelly told herself it was good that Sharon was making an effort.

Bob Prescott whisked the luggage from Mick and placed it on the far side of the kitchen. It was as if an imaginary line had been drawn between Mick and Kelly and the others. Kelly felt helpless as the children were pulled over that line.

"Want a cookie? Want to see the new wallpaper

I hung in your bedrooms?'' Like a child, Sharon sounded eager to please. Yet the children themselves remained quiet.

"We should go.'' Kelly didn't think she could hug the kids goodbye without crying. There were unspoken questions on their faces: *Don't you love us? Don't you want us? Why are you doing this to us?*

The unspoken answers: *Yes! Yes! I don't know!*

Oh Lord, the sweet aroma from the cookies was making her sick. She clutched Mick's arm and found his muscles absolutely rigid.

"We'll see you soon, guys,'' he promised them. "Right, Sharon?''

"Sure, of course.''

Who knew if her glib assurances were sincere?

"Goodbye, Billy. Bye-bye, Amanda.''

They were actually at the door when Billy ran across the room and grabbed the back of Mick's legs. Amanda toddled behind, holding her arms up to Kelly.

"Oh, baby.'' Kelly clutched the child to her. Tears flowed—no use trying to stop them now. Mick put one arm over her shoulder, drawing all four of them into a tight embrace.

"Okay, guys.'' Sharon had clearly had enough. "Doesn't anyone want a cookie?''

Billy was the first to withdraw from the hug. "Yes, Mommy,'' he said. He approached the table as enthused as if she'd offered creamed spinach and cooked cabbage.

Amanda was harder. She latched on to Kelly so tightly that Mick had to pry her off. Kelly felt horrible. She'd earned Amanda's trust, only to abandon her....

Mick held the door open and Kelly stumbled out. The cold air and bright sunlight were a welcome shock. She pulled a tissue from her pocket and mopped up tears, but replacements fell just as quickly. Mick stood slightly away from her, hands in his pockets, chin lifted defiantly.

She knew that what he was trying to defy was his own sadness, his own tears. She tucked her arm in his and drew him toward the car.

Neither of them spoke a word until they were back in their own house, sitting by the fire.

"I just wish I could feel that we'd done the right thing," Mick said.

Already, Kelly had found something the children had left behind. One of Amanda's socks, tucked under a pillow on the sofa. She held the small bit of cotton up to her cheek and nodded. She understood exactly how he felt.

THEY'D MARRIED for the sake of the children. Two months later they were empty nesters.

Mick remained certain it was a temporary state of affairs. "They'll be back," he said one morning, coming upon Kelly at the threshold of the children's rooms.

She'd been staring at the beds, thinking how awful they looked neatly made up. Tousled pillows, a quilt hanging half on the floor, sheets balled up underneath—that was a much more pleasant sight.

Sunday, she and Mick waxed their skis and went to the Canmore Nordic Center. The weather held cold and clear, and snow conditions were excellent. They skied, though, as if it were a job, and covered the track with ruthless determination, until they were so exhausted they could barely manage dinner and a bath before collapsing into bed.

Kelly went straight to sleep, then awoke several hours later, heart pounding, body perspiring. She'd had a different dream this time. Instead of seeing Danny's body and watching it collapse in slow motion in the seconds after she'd shot him, she saw only his face as if in a movie close-up. His eyes were wide-open, the way they'd been in those first few minutes of death, before she'd lowered his lids gently with her fingers.

Oh, Lord, please help me. Kelly blinked a few times and rolled onto her back. She focused on the ceiling, the window, the shapes of the dresser and the chair by the wall. And beside her, Mick slept on his side, his back to her.

This was the real world, *her* world. She had to forget about Danny; that was over, finished.

Kelly shifted onto her side so her back faced Mick's. She didn't want to disturb him; he had to work in the morning. Who knew how she would fill her day and those to come? She pushed aside thoughts of upcoming inquiries. Her lawyer had assured her they would be brief. She wished she could take a job, but as long as she officially remained a member of the RCMP she couldn't work for anyone else.

Volunteer, then? Maybe at the school, in the kindergarten class. That way she could still see Billy—and Amanda, too, when she came with Sharon to pick him up.

The idea was so appealing that suddenly she couldn't wait for morning. She'd go talk to Abby early, before the first bell, and see what she thought. Hopefully, the teacher would be willing—an extra pair of hands always came in handy in a kindergarten class.

Kelly leaned forward to get a look at the clock: only just after three a.m. It would be hours before the alarm went off and she could talk to Mick. She was glad he was sleeping well. Last night he'd tossed and turned, as had she.

How had the children's first night been? She'd longed to phone and ask but hadn't wanted to annoy Sharon. Surely the woman would let them call here if they asked.

Kelly tried to picture the children sleeping right

now in the double bed they shared at Sharon's. She hoped they'd been given baths and were in clean pajamas. And that Sharon was sleeping in *her* bedroom, not on the couch with a six-pack of empties at her feet.

And that she hadn't taken off again and left the kids alone.

Of course she wouldn't do that. She'd only had Billy and Amanda for two nights now, and she'd missed them so much. No doubt she wouldn't risk any behavior that might jeopardize her custody.

But could they count on Sharon being that logical? Kelly knew Mick didn't. What if her boyfriend from Banff suddenly arrived on her doorstep? Or what if she woke up from a bad dream, as Kelly had just done, and reached for the bottle...?

Kelly slipped out of bed. Tormenting herself with thoughts like this was silly. She wasn't going to fall back to sleep, anyway, so she might as well drive over and check things out.

The house was so quiet and cold. Kelly gathered her jeans and sweater from the chair where she'd left them last night. The room was dark with the curtains drawn tight. She swiped the floor with her hand and encountered a pair of Mick's socks. They would do.

She dressed in the bathroom, avoiding her image in the mirror. There was nothing wrong with what she was doing. It was a little paranoid, perhaps, but that was all. She let herself out the front door and crunched through the snow in her hiking boots. She shivered as she started the truck, then went outside to unplug the block heater and coil the extension cord neatly by the garage door.

A blast of wind sent snow tumbling from the roof down on her head, and she brushed away the dry crystals with hands already stiff from the cold. How she missed her RCMP regulation storm coat. The insulated parka was the warmest thing she'd ever worn. When she'd moved out of her basement apartment, she'd packed all her work clothes into several large boxes. Right now, they were in Mick's basement, against the wall, behind her exercise area.

The provincial fatality inquiry was scheduled to begin next week. Her lawyer had called her to prepare her for her testimony. When the hearings were finally over, when her name was cleared, she'd be handing in those boxes, terminating a career that she'd loved until the day she'd been put to the test and discovered she just didn't have what it took....

She slid behind the wheel, started the vehicle and concentrated on driving. The thermometer in her truck told her the temperature had dropped to minus forty overnight. No wonder the steering was so stiff.

As she pulled up in front of Sharon's house, all the windows were dark and a constant stream of white smoke flowed from the chimney. In weather this cold, furnaces ran practically full-time.

Leaving the engine running, she put the truck into park and lowered two of the windows a half-inch each. She felt a little surreal, encased in the small, warm cab, looking out at the frozen landscape around her. The evergreens were frosted white; snow was piled in all the yards and packed smooth along the road. Inside all the tiny little wooden houses were families, presumably fast asleep.

The children *were* safe. Sharon's car was parked in its usual space. The house was quiet and dark. On impulse, Kelly left her truck and went closer to check. She peered in the living room window. As usual the curtains weren't drawn. The sofa was empty; there was no sign of bottles or cans of alcohol.

She walked around to the kitchen side—the light over the stove had been left on and she saw clearly the remains of a fast-food dinner on the table—but again no trace of alcohol.

A wooden gate gave access to the backyard, but here the falling grade made it impossible for her to get a peek into any of the bedroom windows.

Which was, perhaps, just as well.

Feeling a trifle foolish, Kelly went back to her truck. The kids were fine; she was crazy to be worried. She went to shift the truck into drive, but instead turned on the radio. An early-morning breakfast show was starting in Calgary. She might as well sit and listen for a while....

CHAPTER SIXTEEN

MICK LEANED HIS SHOULDER against the cold windowpane. It was five-thirty in the morning and he was scared witless. He had no idea where Kelly was. All he knew was that her side of the bed had been empty when he'd reached for her in his sleep. He'd turned on the bedside lamp and noticed her clothes from last night were missing. Now he could see that her truck was no longer parked outside his house.

Wife comes to senses—regrets hasty marriage.

That had to be it. She'd gone home to her sister's, to Cathleen and Dylan's B and B. It was finally over.

Mick went back to the bedroom and pulled on a pair of sweatpants. He searched for the clean socks he'd worn after his shower last night, but couldn't find them. Perhaps he'd put them in the hamper out of habit. As he dug in his drawer for a new pair, he agonized over what to do about Kelly.

It was dark outside; the sun wouldn't rise for hours. He couldn't call the lodge yet. He'd wake everyone in the house, and if Kelly wasn't there, he'd only get them all worried.

But where else could she be? She'd given up the

lease on her basement apartment and she had no office.

He went back to the kitchen, where making coffee kept his body, if not his mind, busy for a few minutes. Kelly's physical safety wasn't an issue. She was a capable woman, an experienced driver, and she'd left of her own free will.

Because she didn't want to be with him anymore. The reason was self-evident. Their life was so different with the kids gone. *Temporarily* gone. Every cell in his body told him Sharon was going to trip up again. Eventually. And it would be his job to catch the kids before they fell with her.

Mick poured out a cup of the fresh brew and returned to his post by the living room window. His marriage to Kelly had begun as a strange proposition. They'd gone into it for the sake of the children, and on this point it had been an absolute success. No way could he have done so well on his own with the kids these past few months.

It was a success on other levels, too, though obviously Kelly didn't agree. She *seemed* happy, but he'd learned she kept a lot of her deeper feelings to herself. Perhaps she'd had a man in her life before the fiasco with Danny. If so, she might regret...

No. Remembering their lovemaking, he couldn't believe Kelly loved another man. Still, his stomach twisted and turned, rejecting the acidic note in the fresh coffee.

He'd entered into this arrangement with the noble intention of making their relationship last. But that had been damn simplistic. Relationships were demanding, fragile entities. Most of all they were packed with emotions, while his focus had been entirely on the logical.

Cupid had had the last laugh on him. He couldn't imagine a woman more perfect for him than Kelly. She had fit into his life and the children's as if she'd always belonged. Never before had he known the pleasure of sharing meals, evenings, his bed, with someone who seemed to genuinely care what he thought and how he felt.

The idea that she might have left for good—well, it was painful. He felt lonely just thinking about it. Funny, when he'd spent so much of his life on his own, that the prospect of having his house to himself again should fill him with such dread.

Mick tried to assess his feelings objectively. Wanting to be with her all the time, dreaming about making love with her when he was supposed to be working on a story, imagining her reaction when he anticipated telling her a new piece of gossip or a funny joke…

He loved her. That had to be it.

Then, why did he still hold back emotionally from her? He knew that he did. Knew, too, that she sensed his reserve and was hurt by it. It could be that men like him were only capable of so much feeling.

In this case his restraint might be just as well. 'Cause if she was leaving him—

A sound from the road drew his attention back to the real world. She'd returned! Immediately, the pain in his gut eased. He watched her drive into her spot in front of the house, then edge out from behind the wheel. Before coming inside, she plugged the extension cord into her block heater, then brushed some loose snow from her mittens.

He went to the front door and opened it wide. Her long hair didn't appear to have been combed, and she wore her ski clothes from yesterday. But with her cheeks flushed from the cold, she was beautiful. Absolutely beautiful.

"You came back." It was all he could think to say.

"Of course." She slid into the house, into his arms, into his mind. "Isn't this where I belong?"

MICK HAD THOUGHT Kelly's idea of volunteering at the kindergarten was excellent, so at eight-thirty Kelly went to the school to speak to Abby. The teacher was keen and suggested that Kelly start the next day, Tuesday.

Kelly returned home in better spirits. She went for a twenty-minute run—it was too cold to be out any longer—and then descended to the basement to lift weights. She'd just gotten out of the shower and was about to dress to meet Mick for lunch, when the phone rang.

She unwound the towel from her head. "Hello?"

"Kelly? It's Abby."

Responding to the edgy tone in the kindergarten teacher's voice, Kelly sank onto the carpet. "Is Billy all right?"

"He's fine. Kelly, I'm calling about your offer to help out in class." Abby's words starting coming faster. "It's a really generous offer, and I appreciate it, but when I mentioned it to the principal, she suggested we check with Sharon, and I'm sorry to say—"

"Oh, I can imagine what Sharon's reaction was." Kelly tried not to feel bitter. Sharon had very good reason not to like her. But this was such a blow. She'd so looked forward to seeing Billy tomorrow and making sure he was doing okay.

"I am sorry, Kelly."

"I know. Thanks, anyway." Kelly hung up the phone but couldn't find the energy to stand. Instead, she drew in her knees and wrapped her arms around them.

What was she going to do now?

"MAYBE YOU SHOULD'VE married Abby after all."

Mick stopped eating. Kelly, sitting opposite him at the kitchen table, hadn't touched the Chinese takeout he'd picked up on the way home from work.

Kelly had canceled their lunch; he'd wanted to make sure she ate a decent dinner. She had a bathrobe wrapped around her. And from the puffiness around her eyes, he suspected she'd been crying.

Too bad the school had decided against letting her volunteer. He felt pretty bitter toward Sharon about that. When *her* life had been on the rocks, she'd been only too quick to accept help from him and Kelly. Denying Kelly this one, small pleasure was pure mean-spiritedness.

"Why do you think I should've married Abby?" Kelly twirled one of the wooden chopsticks like a miniature baton. "Sharon wouldn't have the same prejudices against her that she has against me."

"Fortunately, I didn't need to take Sharon's opinions into account when I decided who I wanted for my wife."

The chopstick stilled. "But you only married because you needed someone for the kids."

Mick slit open a packet of plum sauce for his spring roll. He didn't like the direction this conversation was taking. Was Kelly questioning his commitment? Or simply looking for an escape hatch for herself?

"I guess that's the way I saw it at the beginning. But it's become a bit more complicated than that."

"Oh?"

Still not sure of Kelly's motivation, he tried to be diplomatic. "I feel we're extraordinarily compatible.

I don't know if I've ever enjoyed anyone's company the way I enjoy yours.''

"Same. Plus, the sex is pretty good."

He grinned. "The sex is great." He considered a further confession, and decided he should make it. "I never felt that way about Abby. I didn't even want to kiss her, let alone make love with her."

"Abby's a lovely woman."

He shook his head. "For the right man she'd be perfect. I found her too perky, too exhaustingly…perky."

"Note to myself—don't be too perky around Mick. I'd say I'm doing a good job of it today." She touched a hand to her unkempt hair, then glanced down at her robe.

Mick pushed away his plate. He'd had enough food. "You're beautiful as always."

"Come on, Mick. I *have* seen myself in the mirror a time or two today."

"If you don't think you look great, you're not focusing on the right things. Come here, I'll show you." He pulled her up from the chair and took her to the full-length mirror in their bedroom. Standing behind her, he gazed at their reflections. Kelly's eyes were downcast, as if she couldn't risk even one tiny glance.

"Look at this hair," he began, filling both of his hands with its weight. "Lustrous and clean and it smells fantastic." He pulled it back from her face.

"Cathleen and Maureen are both stunning, but you inherited the best bones in your family. You must see what I mean." He brushed his fingertips from her chin, along her jaw and up to her cheeks and then her eyes. "Next, your lips. Not too fat, and with the most beautiful curve when you smile."

Kelly rolled her eyes.

"I'm not kidding. And speaking of curves..." He eased her bathrobe down her shoulders, and his body automatically tightened. "I love the line of your neck and the athletic firmness of your arms."

He slid his hands down her shoulders, pushing the bathrobe lower and lower, until her breasts and her slender waist were exposed. He'd suspected she was naked beneath all that terry-cloth. Confirmation sent his desire soaring.

She tried to twist away from the mirror. "Mick, this is embarrassing."

"No, watch," he insisted. "Can't you see how beautiful you are? Just looking at you makes me so crazy I almost can't stand it." He pressed into her so she'd know just *how* crazy.

He put his hands to the tie at her waist. The simple knot easily came undone. A second later she stood completely naked.

"Your legs are outstanding," he said, his hands gliding over the smooth skin of her hips. "Look."

"They're too bulky."

"They're sexy," he insisted. "Just like the rest

of you." He bent to kiss her neck. He loved touching her with the bonus of watching himself touch her in the wooden framed mirror.

"Mick... Mick..."

He was kissing the top of her shoulder, but paused at the desperation in her voice. "You're not asking me to stop?"

"Stop?" She made a sound that was half laugh, half groan. "Oh, Mick, no. That's not what I was going to say at all. I just think we should move to the bed."

"Let me carry you." He put an arm behind her knees, the other across her back. As he swung her up, he noticed the reflection of her feet flash across the mirror.

"So that's where my socks went to."

THE PROVINCIAL FATALITY inquiry into Danny's death took place at the beginning of February in Calgary. Kelly had been dreading her court appearance, but with Mick staunchly by her side, it wasn't too bad.

He must love me, she thought, as she considered how difficult it had to be for him to listen to the testimony regarding his brother. Mick's feelings for Danny ran deep.

As, apparently, did Mick's feelings for her. Yet something was missing, something she couldn't put words to for herself, let alone explain to Mick. She tried with Poppy one afternoon.

Poppy was baking heart-shaped cookies for Valentine's Day. She wanted to perfect the recipe for her cookbook. After the family had their fill, she'd take the extras to the kindergarten, as she often did with her surplus baking.

Kelly picked up one freshly frosted cookie and had a nibble. Her mouth filled with the flavors of butter, vanilla and strawberry. Poppy had used strawberry juice to color the frosting pink.

"You love Mick, so what's the problem?" Poppy asked.

"He acts like he loves me, too, but he never says it."

"Some men find words very difficult," Poppy replied.

"Mick's a journalist! He *works* with words."

"He works with *facts*."

"Good point." Kelly sighed. She understood that Mick had dealt with his difficult childhood by pulling inward. Other than Harvey Tomchuk and, on that one occasion, Rose Strongman, very few people in his life had reached out to him. It stood to reason that he would find it difficult to open his heart.

But her heart was so open she was afraid it would burst. How much longer could she hold back what she was feeling inside?

"BILLY, HONEY, wake up."

Billy tried to push the sound away. He was so, so tired.

"Come on, Billy. We're going to a party. It's going to be lots of fun, you'll see."

A party? He opened his eyes, but it was still dark and he felt confused. His mother sat on the edge of the bed. She had her hair all fancied up like she did when she was going out. And the smell… Oh, no, the smell. He recognized it from the days when she used to cuddle up in bed with him after one of her bad dreams.

That smell meant she was getting sick again.

"No, Mommy, please…"

But she flicked on the light. "Brian phoned me from Banff. He wants to see me again. Isn't that good news? Be a good boy, Billy, and get your sister into the car for me."

"But we're in our pajamas!"

"That's okay. You don't need to change. We're just going to Brian's house. There'll be a bed where you can sleep."

"But I want to sleep in *this* bed."

"Shape up, Billy, okay? Do you want me to leave you and Amanda alone? You know I can't do that. You *must* remember what happened last time."

Oh, boy. Billy felt wide-awake now. He checked out Amanda. She was sleeping like a hedgehog, all curled up on herself.

"I'm going to put on my lipstick and get in the car. I expect you and your sister to be ready in one minute. Got that?"

He did. "Come on, Mandy, you have to wake up."

Of course Amanda only wanted to sleep, the way he had. He half dragged her off the bed, then led her to the bathroom. He'd better make sure she went to pee or she might have an accident in the car.

By the time they were finished with the toilet, Amanda had woken up a little. She was able to walk to the kitchen, where their mother waited.

"Don't bother with boots or mittens," she said. "But you'd better wear a coat. It's fifteen below zero out there."

Billy felt frozen solid the minute he stepped outside. He held his sister's hand as they made their way to the car in their pajamas with the built-in feet, which Kelly had given them. The engine was running, and inside, the air was thick and warm as a quilt.

"Come on, Mandy, I'll put you in your car seat."

"Oh, forget about that thing, Billy. Why don't you ride up here with me." His mother patted the front seat.

Billy pretended not to hear. He got his sister into the seat, then did up the buckle thingy. Then he put his own seat belt on, tightening it the way Uncle Mick had shown him.

"Oh, fine, be a pooper," his mother said. She turned the radio up loud, then started driving.

Minutes went by. Outside his window, it was so dark. Only occasionally did he spot the lights from a passing vehicle. When he did, they mostly belonged to big semi-trucks.

Billy's head jerked sideways, and he struggled for a deep breath of air. It was so hot in here, and now his mother was smoking. He hated the smell of that stuff and wanted to open a window. But he was afraid to make her mad.

The song on the radio changed. It must've been one his mom liked, because she turned the radio even louder and started singing. Billy saw her reach for another cigarette.

"Shit. Where did I put that—"

The car lurched, and Billy felt as if he was flying sideways. The dotted line on the road was gone. He heard the squeal of brakes, then his mother's cry.

"Oh, Jesus, Jesus, Jesus!"

The seat belt at Billy's waist burned. The car kept moving. What was happening?

Uncle Mick! Kelly! Help me!

CHAPTER SEVENTEEN

KELLY WAS AWAKE when the phone rang at one in the morning. She tried to grab it before it bothered Mick. Probably it was just a wrong number. Late-night calls often were.

"Constable Shannon." Jeez, her brain must be addled. She was speaking as if she were at work. "Sorry, Mick and Kelly's. Who's calling, please?"

"This is Betty Gruber from the Banff Regional Hospital."

Kelly dropped her feet to the floor. All her loved ones flashed through her mind. Her sisters, her friends...the children. *Please, no...*

"I need to speak with Mick Mizzoni. I have him listed as the uncle of Billy and Amanda Mizzoni."

Mick was now awake, staring at her with dread. "What is it, Kel?"

She handed him the receiver. "Not good, Mick. It's the hospital...Billy and Mandy—" She choked on the words, then moved over on the bed to hug Mick while he spoke.

"How are they?" he asked. Then added, "And their mother?"

Kelly squeezed him and prayed. *Let them be okay. I'll do anything if they're just okay.*

Mick placed a hand over the mouthpiece to whisper, "Sharon and the kids were in a car accident. The kids are all right...just minor injuries." Then he returned to his call with more questions. "What happened? What time was it? Where exactly?"

Minor injuries. Kelly played the phrase over and over in her mind. The kids were alive; they weren't badly hurt. But what about Sharon?

The phone call seemed to last forever. Kelly pressed her face against Mick's bare shoulder, taking in the smell of his warm skin. She should be getting dressed, maybe make some coffee for the drive, but she felt she couldn't let go of Mick—that if she did, everything truly would fall apart.

Mick dug for information with all the persistence and experience his years in journalism had given him. Nothing from his side of the conversation, however, gave her any clue about how Sharon had fared. If she'd been injured, in a way it would be Kelly's fault. As so many things were, because they dated back, every one of them, to that awful afternoon when she'd made a choice between two lives.

Her sister's and Danny Mizzoni's.

She'd played God and chosen her sister. That her actions had been within the law, that they were what was expected from her in her role as an RCMP officer, didn't change the facts.

Finally Mick hung up.

"Tell me," she said.

"In the car, okay?" He was already beyond her touch, reaching into drawers for clothes. He threw her some underwear, jeans, a shirt. Kelly dressed, her mind numb.

"But the kids are okay, right?"

"Scrapes and bruises, that sort of thing. Nothing more serious than that, or so they assure me."

Mick snatched his keys and wallet from the nightstand. "Ready?"

She nodded.

They grabbed coats from the hooks by the back door and boots from the rubber mat beneath. Mick had parked in the garage, so his car started easily despite the cold. Soon they were en route to Banff, and Kelly dared the question she most feared.

"Sharon? Was she driving? Is she all right, too?"

Mick brushed a hand over his face. "Yeah, she was driving, and I suppose she's okay. She lost the baby, though."

MICK DIDN'T SHAKE the irrational fear that the nurse had lied to him over the phone and that the kids were actually hurt, or worse, until he and Kelly ran into Emerg and saw them waiting. Their pale, serious faces broke into smiles of relief that couldn't begin to match his.

"Uncle Mick!"

"Kewwy!" Amanda ran into Kelly's arms, while Mick scooped Billy into the air. The boy felt so tiny, so fragile.

Kelly examined an abrasion on the little girl's cheek. "Poor baby."

"The car landed sideways," Billy explained. "The window broke and some of the glass cut her face."

"How about you, Billy?" Mick asked. He put Billy down but kept a hand on the boy's head, needing the contact to reassure himself the child was alive and relatively well.

"I got bruises." Billy lifted his pajama top. "See?"

The dark marks looked violent and ugly, and they would be worse tomorrow. "That's from your seat belt," he said. "I'm glad you were wearing it, Billy. Did your mother strap you in?"

"No, she told me not to bother, so I put it on myself. And I buckled Mandy in her car seat, too."

"You probably saved your sister's life." Mick sucked in a breath, fighting against the blackness of a rage that would do no one any good.

What the hell had Sharon been thinking? Over the phone the nurse had given him the main facts regarding the accident. Sharon had been driving drunk, and veered off the road while searching for her cigarettes. Fortunately, she'd had a shallow ditch and vegetation to stop her rather than the sheer drop on the other side of the road. Her negligence was unbelievable. Now to find out five-year-old Billy was the only reason the kids had been safely strapped into their seats!

Bloody hell! What if Billy had been too tired or too confused to put on the seat belts?

He breathed in another lungful of antiseptic hospital air and told himself to get a grip. "Where's your mother now?" he asked.

The nurse who'd been attending the children answered. "Mrs. Mizzoni has been admitted for observation. The children haven't seen her since they arrived in the ambulance. The doctors don't think it's advisable at this time, although you may have a few minutes if you wish."

Mick didn't wish. He didn't trust himself in the same room as that woman. Sharon, who hadn't been wearing a seat belt, had suffered many scrapes and cuts, as well as internal damage. Now Danny's baby was gone, his brother's final legacy.

Mick was surprised when Kelly spoke up. She'd been so quiet, pale and trembling, still holding Amanda, the little girl's arms wrapped around her neck.

"I'll talk to her," she said. "Here, Mick. You take Mandy."

KELLY FOLLOWED the nurse's directions to Sharon's room. She found the traumatized woman in the first bed by the door, the thin sheet meeting her cotton hospital gown at her waist. Her eye makeup was smeared; her hair was limp and greasy looking. She turned as Kelly entered the room, but her blank expression didn't change.

"Your sister will be here shortly," Kelly said, relaying the message the nurse had just given her. "How are you feeling?"

Sharon didn't answer. She looked away from Kelly to the wall opposite her bed.

"I'm sorry about the baby."

Sharon plucked at the bed sheet, as if removing flecks of lint. "It's probably for the best. I couldn't have raised that kid on my own. Look at Billy and Amanda...I couldn't even—" She stopped and brushed down the sheet, then finally glanced back at Kelly. "I should've had an abortion months ago."

The words sounded callous. Except that tears had started flowing from Sharon's exhausted eyes. Despite herself, Kelly was moved.

"What can I do, Sharon? Is there anything you need?"

"How about a streak of good luck?" Sharon pulled her hair back from her face, then laughed dryly, which seemed to cause some pain. She put her hands to her middle and grimaced. "This has been one of those years. One bad thing after another..."

Kelly's sympathy fizzled. "You were driving

drunk, Sharon. Do you really blame the accident on bad luck?''

''You're such a prude, you know that? I only had a few beers.''

Kelly said nothing. Sharon's blood-alcohol had been well above the legal limit, which suggested the woman was not telling the truth.

''Fortunately, Billy and Amanda weren't seriously hurt.'' It was the most generous thing she could think of to say under the circumstances.

''Yeah.'' Sharon's voice was dull, as if she didn't even care.

Suddenly, Kelly realized she couldn't stomach another minute of the woman's company. She'd come out of a sense of duty, intending to offer comfort. Mick had been wise to stay away. Sharon had learned nothing from this experience. She clearly wasn't prepared to accept responsibility for her actions.

Just as she would never admit that Danny's death might be partly his fault.

It certainly was more than *bad luck* that Danny had carried an illegal handgun. Or that thousands of dollars' worth of illegal drugs were found on his property.

Probably if Sharon's baby had survived and been born with fetal alcohol syndrome, Sharon would have blamed that on bad luck, too, instead of on her own drinking problem.

Disgusted, Kelly turned to leave. Sharon stopped her with a final request.

"You'll take care of my kids?"

For a beat, Kelly was silent. Did Sharon mean for the night, a week or forever? She decided the answer didn't really matter.

"Of course we will." She closed the door and went to rejoin her family.

ON MONDAY, Mick was back in his office, working on the layout of the front page for that week, when a call came through from the mayor.

"What's the matter with you?" Max Strongman demanded. "Can't you control that family of yours? That drunken whore's accident is the talk of the town."

"Appreciate your concern, Mayor. Billy and Amanda are just fine."

Silence. Then a series of curses. "Don't get smart with me. I thought I warned you that I wanted those kids taken care of. If you won't do it, then I will."

Mick adjusted some papers on his desk. His dislike and distrust of Strongman had never been stronger.

"I'm just as concerned as you are. Kelly and I have them now, and we're going to do everything we can to keep them."

Despite Kelly's reluctance, he'd called her sister Maureen in Calgary on Sunday. Maureen thought they stood a good chance of winning a custody battle. At the first sign of trouble from Sharon, he would instruct Maureen to go ahead.

Sharon had messed up with those kids for the last time. He was determined—even more determined than Max Strongman—that she not be given the chance to make another foolish mistake where their welfare was concerned.

"Just know one thing, Mick, my boy," Strongman said. "I expect you to keep those kids out of trouble. And I'll be watching to make sure you do."

MICK FOUND IT HARD to work after Strongman's call. Then impossible, an hour later, when Springer gave him a buzz with a special update. After hanging up, Mick stared out his office window, unable to appreciate the news or the view. The lengthy investigation into her actions the day Danny had been killed was finally over. Both the internal investigation and the provincial inquiry had commended her actions. He wished he could feel simply happy for Kelly. But his emotions were much more complicated.

Not that he wasn't relieved for her. Of course he was. Kelly had always been adamant that she wouldn't return to police work, but having her name vindicated would surely be an enormous relief. Maybe now her nightmares would stop and she could finally start sleeping through the night again.

Defying his gloomy mood, Mick left the office early and picked up flowers from the shop down the street. He pondered the selections available in the glass-windowed refrigerator and realized he had no idea what kind of blossoms she preferred. She'd carried white roses at their wedding. He would buy her some of those.

Hard to believe it was his own house he walked into fifteen minutes later. Instead of the quiet he'd grown accustomed to in the month the kids had been away, he heard a comforting medley of voices coming from the kitchen. As soon as he appeared in the doorway, Billy and Amanda threw themselves at him. Kelly stood back, smiling.

One glance at her face and he knew Springer had called her with the news.

"Congratulations," he said, kissing her on the mouth and then passing her the bouquet.

"Thank you, Mick."

She seemed to like his choice of blooms. She put them in a vase, while he hugged the kids again, then checked Amanda's scrapes and Billy's bruises.

"Hey, these are looking better."

Billy nodded. "We're building a zoo in our bedroom. Want to see?"

"In a second, Billy. I'd like to speak with Kelly first."

"Sure." He nodded and ran off, Amanda not far behind.

From his perch on the edge of the counter, Mick watched Kelly fuss with the arrangement. Her smile gave him a pleasant buzz in his chest.

"You look happy."

"We've had *such* a nice day. We made pancakes for breakfast, then went for a walk to the playground. It was too cold to stay long, but I gave them each a swing. Then I dropped Billy off at kindergarten. Do you know he missed about ten days when he was staying at Sharon's?"

Mick shook his head. "I guess during bad weather she didn't bother going out."

"I'm so glad we have them back. And now that the investigation is over... Well, it just seems that things are looking up for us, doesn't it."

Ignoring the dull ache in his gut, he went to her and locked his hands around her waist. She was relieved. He was glad this final pressure had been eased from her conscience. Kelly didn't deserve to suffer. She'd paid her dues.

"Strongman called me today," he said. "About the accident. He wasn't worried about the kids, just annoyed that they'd been involved in such a disgraceful spectacle."

"Oh, that man..."

"He is *long* overdue for a fall."

The stove timer buzzed, and Kelly edged out of his embrace to take a cake from the oven. He noticed she had salad fixings soaking in cold water in the sink and offered to chop them for dinner.

"Why don't you check out the kids' zoo first?"

He was just heading down the hall, when the phone rang. Kelly held up her wet hands. He nodded and grabbed the receiver.

It was a nurse from the hospital in Banff. "Have you seen or heard from Sharon Mizzoni?" she asked.

A noose of dread tightened around his throat. He glanced at Kelly, realized she would have told him if Sharon had contacted her, and focused back on the call. "No."

"She seems to have left the hospital without checking out. No one's seen her since her sister came to visit early this afternoon."

"Have you tried calling Carrie?"

"We did, but there was no answer. It's not that Mrs. Mizzoni is in any danger, but the doctor was going to prescribe some medication…"

"I understand. I'll let you know if we hear from her." He settled the phone back in the console and reflected on his earlier feeling of contentment. He wished he could have enjoyed it at least a few hours longer.

"What is it, Mick?"

"Sharon slipped out of the hospital sometime this afternoon. The nurse I spoke to thinks she's proba-bly with her sister, although she can't be sure because there's been no answer at Carrie's. I suppose Sharon could have gone anywhere, really.''

"And not left any word... Isn't that just like her? The woman is so irresponsible." Kelly let her frustration show in a drawn-out sigh. "I suppose we should try to find her and make sure she's okay."

"After dinner I'll check out the bungalow."

"And I'll try her sister's again. Although maybe she's with that boyfriend of hers."

Mick nodded. "She couldn't have gone far. Her car was totaled in the accident."

BUT SHARON HAD gone far, at least according to her sister when Kelly finally was able to reach her, shortly after tucking in the kids that night.

"Sharon's split. Headed for B.C., I think," Carrie said.

"But *why?*" Kelly propped the phone between her ear and her shoulder as she tidied up the dishes from the bedtime snack. Sharon hadn't even said goodbye to the children.

"Told me she was sick of her life. She needed to get away from Canmore and the goddamn mountains—her words—so she could think straight."

"But her car was totaled..."

"She took mine. I don't really mind."

Kerry noted Carrie's word choice and caught the implication. "She *stole* your car?"

"Not really. Just borrowed without asking."

"You could press charges."

"Hell, that old clunker wasn't even worth as much as Sharon's Buick. She'll probably send me the insurance money when the claim comes through."

Kelly wasn't so sure, but if Carrie didn't know her own sister by now... "What about the kids? Did she leave a message for them?"

"She just said to get Mick to look after them. She said he would."

"Of course he will. *We* will."

"Well, then. That's okay, isn't it?"

Carrie sounded as though there was nothing at all strange about any of this. As if Kelly was the peculiar one for asking all the questions. Kelly couldn't imagine her sisters being so blasé if *she* decided to peel out of her hospital bed early, steal a car and abandon her children.

"Talk to you later, then?"

Before Carrie could hang up, Kelly gathered her thoughts. "There is one more thing, Carrie. If you hear from Sharon, she should get in touch with the hospital. Apparently she left without her prescription."

Carrie disconnected the call with a vague promise about the medication, just as Mick came through the door to the garage.

"No one's at the bungalow," he said.

"I know. I just talked to Sharon's sister. She's

run off, Mick. She wants us to have Billy and Amanda.''

Mick stopped brushing stray snowflakes from the shoulders of his jacket. ''For how long?''

Kelly shrugged. ''Forever would be nice.''

He plopped down on the bench by the door and tugged at his boots. Once they were off, he just sat there. ''God knows I'm happy to have the kids, but that woman is driving me crazy. She's about as stable as uranium.''

''True. But the important thing is that we have Billy and Amanda again. Right?''

Mick didn't answer at first. He was watching her and his gaze held an objective quality that made her distinctively uneasy. What was he searching for?

''You don't mind that she's taken off?'' he asked.

''Of course not, since it means we keep the children. Of course, I feel bad for Billy and Amanda. They'll be confused at first, and probably sad that she didn't say goodbye.''

Kelly stopped talking. She had a feeling that Mick's question held a subtext she hadn't caught. Was he worried that she didn't want the children? That the prospect of having them forever frightened her?

''This is why we got married in the first place,'' she reminded him. ''Mick, you don't have to question my commitment to these children.''

''To the children? No.'' Mick sighed, then hung

up his jacket and aligned his boots carefully on the rubber mat. "Are they in bed?"

He'd gone from studying her like a textbook to avoiding her eyes completely. He was tidying up the toys now—something she'd been meaning to do after this call.

"Yes. They're sleeping."

"Good." He had his back to her, working away from her. "I have some reading to do in my office."

"Fine." There went her expectations of sharing a cup of coffee by the fire, then watching the news and going to bed together. Mick's body language screamed, *Stay away!* But she had no clue why that should be.

She understood his frustration and anger at Sharon. But right now, this weird exchange was all about them as a couple. She was sure of it. More than anything, Kelly wanted to follow him to his office and ask what was wrong.

So do it, she urged herself. Mick was at the glass door that led from the living room to his office. All she had to do was call out his name....

Kelly curled her fingers around one of Billy's plastic dump trucks as Mick's name remained stuck at the back of her throat. If she asked him to talk, what would she say? That he was acting distant? But he would only remind her of the terms of their marriage.

She and Mick had started with a slip of paper and

two rings, then graduated to sharing a bed. But their hearts hadn't made a commitment yet. And that didn't seem to be in the cards for the immediate future.

CHAPTER EIGHTEEN

"Ow! DAMN IT!" Mick grabbed his bare foot and leaned against the stairwell wall. Pain throbbed all the way to his ankle. Embedded in the fleshy pad of skin on the ball of his foot he found a tiny Lego piece.

"Billy!"

How could something so little hurt so bloody much?

Kelly, passing on her way up the stairs, a glass of water in her hand, paused to take a look. Unfortunately, there was no blood or gore to impress her.

"Why the hell is Billy always leaving these damn things on the floor?"

There was no sympathy in Kelly's cool perusal. "He's five, Mick. Get a grip. He's also almost asleep, so please try not to yell any more."

Mick choked back an angry reply. He knew he'd been on edge all day. Actually, all week. He'd done his best to hide his mood from the kids, which meant Kelly was getting the brunt of it. He could tell she was feeling confused and hurt by his behavior. So he'd taken to retreating to his home office after the kids were in bed, to spare her the discomfort of his company.

Contemplating the computer on his desk and the neat stack of papers on the tray beside it, he wondered if life was ever going to improve. How long could he and Kelly continue to live like this? Personally, he didn't think he could stand it much longer.

Mick noticed a file drawer was partially open, and he slammed it shut with more force than necessary. The bang echoed in the slumbering house.

During the short period the kids had lived with Sharon, he'd been pretty sure Kelly had assessed their relationship and found it wanting. Now that Billy and Amanda were back, she seemed happy again, but he wished that *he alone* could have made her happy. Was that incredibly selfish and unrealistic of him?

The thing was, he wanted to believe that he had come to mean something to Kelly, that she was with him for reasons beyond guilt and obligation.

But then, he had his own burden of guilt to bear. Lately, he couldn't get thoughts of his brother out of his head. Probably it was because the inquiries had come to an end; the public and the law now considered his brother's death "Case Closed."

Not that he'd wished for any other outcome. The problem was, he didn't know what he felt. Only that somehow Danny had been cheated. And he, Mick, had been the one to gain.

Mick forced himself to stay in his home office until he was certain Kelly was asleep. Then he crawled into bed beside her, careful not to disturb her. By the time he awoke on Saturday morning, he was alone. The running shoes she usually kept under the chair by the nightstand were gone. Mick blinked, then glanced at the clock radio. Six–forty-five. It was the weekend, but he supposed he might as well get up.

The radio alarm clicked on while he was brushing his teeth. He returned to the room in time to hear the last stanza of a song by the Rolling Stones.

"Too damn early for this stuff." He switched the alarm off and got dressed. Feeling a little like soiled laundry himself, he started a load of whites in the washer, then went to the kitchen to make coffee.

Kelly breezed in the side door, just as Amanda waddled into the kitchen, demanding her favorite cereal.

"It's warming up out there," she said, tugging off her toque and the scarf she wore wrapped around her mouth. "Where's Billy?"

"Coming." The small boy's voice echoed from down the hall. A second later, Billy trudged into the kitchen, pulled a chair across the floor so he could reach the bowls and picked out his own box of cereal.

Now, as always, the five-year-old's maturity astounded Mick.

The four of them ate in relative harmony. Guilty of being in a lousy mood all week, Mick cast about for an idea to make it up to them.

"How about we go sledding," he suggested. "It's not that cold and there's plenty of fresh snow." He glanced at Kelly to check that his plan was okay.

She nodded, then turned away. Apparently she wouldn't be joining them.

"Good idea, Uncle Mick! We can use our new sleds." Billy, at least, was excited about the idea.

Mick helped the kids get dressed and brush their teeth, leaving Kelly to tidy the kitchen. While the little ones were struggling into snowsuits, he grabbed the sleds from the garage.

Kelly stood at the door, watching him snap the buckles of the kids' car seats. She waved as he backed out the driveway, and blew kisses to the children. He told himself he was being ridiculous to care so much that she hadn't wanted to come. She had Billy and Amanda full-time all week. Probably she craved a little peace and quiet.

Or else she'd opted out of the activity because she didn't want to be around *him.*

KELLY KNEW IT WAS SILLY to feel bad that Mick hadn't asked her along on the sledding excursion. If she'd wanted to go, she should've said so. But she hadn't, so no sense sulking. She'd start a load of laundry, then lift some weights.

She wasn't surprised to find the hamper of dirty clothes missing from the bathroom. Mick had obviously beaten her to the task. She went downstairs and switched the clothes to the dryer, then started a second load. Now she was free to work out.

About to select music for her CD player and start with some arm curls, she noticed the boxes stacked behind her weights. They'd started to get dusty. Had she been here that long already?

She ripped the packing tape off the first one and raised the cardboard flaps. Packed at the top was her forage cap and navy storm coat, both proudly bearing the RCMP crest. Kelly grazed a finger over the embroidered design, then dug lower to find her patrol jacket and several pairs of navy trousers with the distinctive yellow stripes down the side of each leg.

Emotion swept over her like a tantalizing scent she couldn't put a name to. She'd missed these clothes, damn it. Missed the routine of getting dressed in the morning and driving to the detachment, never knowing what surprises the day would reveal.

Kelly repackaged the box, then sank onto the cold cement floor. The relief of having the investigation over, her name cleared, was greater than she'd expected. Not that she'd been led to expect any other outcome, but still, it was nice to know that at least in the eyes of the law she'd done nothing wrong.

Now she thought of the grueling training she'd gone through to be part of a police force recognized as distinctively Canadian throughout the world. To be a member of the Royal Canadian Mounted Police had once meant something very important to her. She glanced back at the box of clothing she'd just repacked.

Maybe it still did. Walking away wasn't going to be as easy as she'd thought.

So what are you going to do, Kelly?

Her entire life was a mess. Just look at her marriage. Her relationship with Mick was getting rockier every day, and she didn't know what to do about it.

Why had he turned so miserable once the kids had moved back in? She knew he loved them and wanted to take care of them. The problem couldn't be Billy and Amanda. Which meant it had to be *her*.

But what had she done wrong? She couldn't think of anything that was different....

Wait a minute. Of course there was something. The inquiry results. Mick's strange mood had started the very day they'd found out. Kelly let out a small moan and covered her face with her hands. Was Mick unhappy with the results of that investigation? Did he resent the fact that she wasn't going to pay any price for having shot his brother?

Oh my Lord, that has to be it.

KELLY HAD FINISHED her workout and folded the first load of laundry by the time Mick and the kids returned. She went to the kitchen, put on the kettle, then waited for them at the door.

They rolled in like snowballs, wet and sticky and white. Billy was laughing at a story Mick was just finishing. Amanda's cheeks were as red as plums and she smiled broadly when she saw Kelly.

"Fun!" she said, clapping her mitts together.

Startled by the first word she'd ever heard the three-year-old utter, Kelly needed a few seconds to respond.

"You *look* like you had fun." She bent to help remove the soggy snowsuit and snow-crusted mittens, dropping kisses on the girl's cold cheeks. A sideways glance revealed that Mick hadn't missed the significance of what had just happened. For the first time since Sharon had left, warmth was exchanged between them.

"I tell you, these kids have no fear," Mick said. "I was worried the hill would be too steep, but all they wanted was to go faster!"

"I raced Uncle Mick and Mandy," Billy said proudly.

"We won! We won!" Amanda said. She danced in a big circle, sprinkling snow from her boots all over the floor.

"Come back here, squirt!" Kelly snagged the happy toddler, whose half-undone snowsuit dragged from the waist. "Let's get these wet clothes off and have some hot chocolate."

"With marshmallows?" Billy asked.

Kelly nodded.

"Marmows?"

"That's right, sweetie." Finally Kelly managed to unsnare the squirming girl from the last of her winter outerwear. She'd throw the lot in the dryer later, but right now she could hear the kettle whistling. As she rose to get the cocoa mix, Mick swooped in on his niece to pick her up and cuddle her to his chest.

"You're beautiful. Did you know that, Amanda?"

The little girl nodded. "Yes. Kewwy told me."

Again Kelly met Mick's gaze. Warmth, laughter, relief…they flowed freely between them, and Kelly felt a dizzying rush of happiness.

Maybe everything was going to work out after all. The children were happy, Amanda was talking again. She couldn't stop herself—she leaned over to kiss Mick's cheek. Anticipating the move, he shifted his face so her lips fell on his mouth.

"Nice," he said, his eyes showing more affection than they had all week.

"Very," she agreed. She moved away to start mixing the hot chocolate. Billy had already located the package of minimarshmallows. Amanda wanted to help, too.

"You can drop in the marshmallows," Kelly said. "Billy, do you want to be the official stirrer?"

He did. Mick dragged two stools to the counter so both children could be up where the action was. Kelly supervised the process with budding optimism for their future together—the four of them. Tonight she'd speak to Mick about her plans to go back to work.

Maybe once they got started, they'd be able to speak about other things, too. The children, their relationship... Maybe she'd been wrong about the reasons for Mick's strange mood this week. And while she didn't expect a declaration of love from him, she did hope they could get back to the way they'd been just one month ago.

Making love, talking, laughing together. Surely she had a right to expect at least that from her patchwork marriage.

MICK HIMSELF BROACHED the topic once the children were asleep that night.

"So what happens now that the investigation is complete? Do you resign or what?" He sat in his favorite chair, feet up.

Kelly had just poured them both coffee. She didn't know why he hadn't escaped to his office tonight, as he had the rest of the week, but she was glad he hadn't.

Settled into her spot on the sofa, she cradled the warm mug in her hands. She'd grown used to Mick's preference for dusky illumination in the evening. The fire flickered in the darkened room, and as usual, the blinds on the large picture window allowed in horizontal lines of pale light from the street lamps outside.

"Interesting you should ask," she said. "I was thinking about my job this afternoon."

"And?"

"After the shooting, the idea of going back seemed out of the question."

"I remember. We talked about that."

"Yes, but now that the moment of decision is here, I find I'm reluctant to quit. Isn't that ironic?"

"What do you mean, reluctant?" Mick's voice resonated with an urgency that jarred the relaxed atmosphere.

Kelly set her mug of coffee near the edge of the table. Careful to keep her tone modulated, she tried to explain. "This is an important decision, Mick."

"But I thought it was one you'd already made."

"You mean you expected I would always stay home full-time with Billy and Amanda?"

Mick waved a hand impatiently. "I never intended to chain you to the house, Kelly. Part-time baby-sitting or day care—I have no problem with that if you find the right job. I've also been considering making special work arrangements with our publisher so that I can spend more time at home."

"That would be great."

He leaned into his chair. "So have you thought about what you'd like to do?"

Kelly reached over to stir her coffee. Wasn't he listening? "I might just go back." She felt a flutter of anxiety when he didn't respond. "Springer called this afternoon, pressing me for a start date, and I'm thinking next week…''

"Are you talking about a desk job?"

"No."

Mick uncoiled his long legs and stood. From her vantage point he appeared very tall, his form almost threatening in the variegated light from the window.

"You're not returning to duty as a patrol officer."

His commanding tone made her frown. "Was that a question, Mick?"

"Did it need to be? Damn it, Kelly, I don't understand."

"It's not that difficult. I've decided to go back to my job." And because he was being so obtuse about it, she added, "I've made up my mind."

Mick paced to the fireplace, then turned, his face now in shadows that flickered and danced in patterns that seemed almost sinister.

"I don't get it," he said. "Surely you see that what you're suggesting is out of the question."

"No, I don't see that. And I'm not *suggesting* anything."

"You're telling. Is that your point?" His mouth twisted bitterly. "I wonder whether they'll give you your old gun back. Would you like that, Kelly? How do you think it'll feel to hold it in your hands again, to carry it against your body?"

A terrible sweat broke out under Kelly's arms and across her back and chest. She fell back into the cushions of the sofa, frightened by the almost diabolical gleam in Mick's eyes. Was it a reflection from the fire or a trick of the shadows? But no, his next words convinced her that he really was trying to hurt her.

"Where will you keep the gun when you come home at night, Kelly? When Billy and Amanda are older, will you tell them that's the very weapon you shot their daddy with?"

"No!" She buried her head in her arms. This wasn't Mick. It couldn't be. He would never say these things.

But he was. And he kept saying them, wouldn't shut up.

"Can't you see it's not right? Don't go back there! This family will never survive if you do."

Kelly stumbled to her feet, holding out one hand as if she could block his words, the awful picture he made standing so stiffly with his face hard, his arms crossed. The urge to flee overpowered her. She had to get out, away from him. Down the hall she fled, to the front door.

"I'm not going to *hurt* you." Mick sounded contemptuous.

What the hell did he think he'd just done? "I finally get it, Mick. God, it took me long enough, but I finally get it."

"What are you talking about?"

"Why you keep that distance between us. You tried. I have to admit you tried. But you can't hold back what you really feel."

"Oh? And what is that?"

"You hate me."

She gulped back a sob, hating *herself* for being so weak. She had to keep talking—better that the words come from her than from him. "Of course you despise me. I killed your brother. No man could be expected to forgive something so terrible."

And she'd been a fool to think he had. She should have known that his logical acceptance of the circumstances of Danny's death had been a cover-up for his true feelings. True feelings he probably hadn't even admitted to himself, until recently. How could he? Mick was a master at avoiding his feelings.

Tears made it hard for her to pick out her coat, to find her keys on the hook. God, this hurt so much, was even worse than those minutes after—

"Where are you going?" Mick took one step forward, then stopped. "You're leaving me, aren't you. For good."

His lashing, hurtful anger dissipated before her eyes. Standing before her suddenly was a regretful, pain-ridden man. And that was almost worse. Because she knew Mick hadn't wanted to blame her. He just couldn't stop himself.

"I don't know what I'm doing, Mick. We've sure dug ourselves into one hell of a hole, haven't we?" She pulled on her gloves with desperate tugs. She needed out, needed the cold, needed the space.

"But the kids…"

Yes. The kids. They were the anchor that would see her through this storm. She had to figure out what was best for them. But she couldn't do that here with Mick, when she wanted him so bad she'd almost sell her soul.

Unfortunately, her soul was no longer available to sell or to keep. She'd lost it, hadn't she, the day she'd killed Danny Mizzoni.

Kelly opened the door. A gust of wind almost blew it out of her hands. "I'll be at the B and B," she called back to Mick.

It was snowing. The cold and the wind tumbled over her, fighting her efforts to move toward her truck. She didn't mind; she was glad for the struggle. The next twenty-four hours were going to be the hardest of her life. If Sharon were in her shoes, she'd head for the bar.

Sadly, Kelly was in Kelly's shoes. And they made for a pretty painful fit these days.

CHAPTER NINETEEN

DRIFTS OF SNOW lay over the highway like speed bumps as Kelly drove to the B and B. Visibility was bad, with the relentless snowfall driving into her windshield. Kelly was glad for the need to concentrate. When she'd parked outside Larch Lodge she was breathing normally again.

But her emotional stability crumbled the moment Poppy's concerned face peeked out the door. The pain she'd been running from surfaced like blood spurting from a wound. By the time she'd made it to the porch, she could hardly see.

"You're crying, love! What is it?"

"Ca-Cathleen and Dylan?"

"They're out visiting friends. Come inside. It's *cold* out there." Poppy reached for her hands and pulled her over the threshold.

Kelly rubbed her eyes, trying to clear her vision. The kitchen was, as always, clean and comfortable and filled with the most amazing scents. She sank into a pine chair, and Poppy sat next to her.

"It's over, Poppy. I can't stay with him anymore."

Poppy sucked in a breath. "Oh, no."

"Yet, there're the children to think of. I *can't* abandon them after all they've been through." She folded her arms on the table and let her head drop. "Lord, it's such a mess. What should I do?"

For once Poppy didn't offer tea or cake. She put her hand on Kelly's back and said, "Maybe you just need to cry for a while."

Kelly couldn't remember ever actually sobbing in front of another person, but no sooner were the words out of Poppy's mouth than tears started again. Her whole body heaved as the pain flowed out of her toward the woman who sat beside her, stroking her shoulders and making soft, comforting noises.

"You poor darling," Poppy said. She left for a moment, then came back with a handful of tissues. "I know how it hurts. Believe me, I know."

"Do you?" Kelly wiped under her eyes, her nose. Poppy never talked about herself, and Kelly had never pried. But of course a woman couldn't reach the age of seventy without having encountered some heartbreak in her life.

"My husband ran out when my son was just a baby."

Kelly hadn't expected this. Somehow she'd always assumed Poppy had never married. "I didn't know you had children."

"Just one. But I was foolish in those days. I've learned a few things since then. I can tell Mick is a good man. Give him a chance, and you'll sort through your problems."

Kelly stared at the pile of damp tissues in her hands. "You wouldn't say that if you'd heard what he said to me tonight. He'll never get over the fact that I killed his brother."

"Don't place too much emphasis on words spoken in the heat of the moment," Poppy advised. She placed her hand once more on Kelly's back, and Kelly immediately felt soothed.

To think that she and her sisters had only known Poppy since the summer was amazing, really. In just a few months they'd all become so close. Kelly put an arm around the elderly lady. "How lucky for us you picked Cathleen's B and B when you came to town, Poppy. I doubt we ever could've survived without you."

"Oh, don't be silly. I haven't done anything."

"You've been wonderful," Kelly insisted. Poppy had filled so many holes in the Shannon sisters' lives that she had to feel like the family minister, or counselor, or even surrogate mother.

"I haven't been wonderful at all," Poppy said. "Actually, I've been rather selfish."

"That's ridiculous."

"Not really." Poppy pulled away from the hug and regarded her frankly. "I'm not writing a cookbook."

Kelly was tired and still distraught. Processing

what Poppy was saying took a few moments. "But you're always testing recipes. And they're all *wonderful.*"

"Thank you. But the real reason I came to Canmore was to get to know you girls."

Kelly stared. Was it her addled brain, or was this conversation really not making any sense?

"Remember the son I was telling you about? He was your father."

Kelly's brain *was* scrambled. She couldn't be hearing right.

"I'm your grandmother, Kelly. That's why I came to Larch Lodge."

"TAKE A GOOD LOOK, kids. This is the house where your dad and I grew up." Mick shielded his eyes from the sun. Hard to believe the old place was still standing. But some enterprising young couple, with more heart than money, had painted the one-story wooden structure with a rainbow assortment of bright colors—turquoise over the walls, pink for the trim, blue on the door and the shutters.

"It's really little," Billy said.

Mick knew it was. Just one bedroom, and all the rooms were tiny.

"Pretty. Flower." Amanda pointed to the painted-on window box under the front window.

"Yes, it is nice, isn't it." But there'd been nothing attractive about the house when he'd grown up here. No curtains hanging from the window in re-laxed pleats, no mat at the front door assuring vis-itors they were welcome.

This house had been a dark and dreary place, and he'd been glad to escape from it. Going off to uni-versity had marked the end of an era for his brother and him. By the time he'd returned to Canmore, their mother was gone and Danny had already met up with Sharon and was entrenched in a lifestyle that revolved around drinking and drugs and small-time crime.

"Were you and Daddy really brothers?" Billy asked him.

"I was your daddy's big brother, just like you are to Mandy." Only, he hadn't done nearly the job of looking after Danny that Billy did for his sister.

Mick herded the kids back into the car. "Let's go downtown for lunch." Stopping here had been a waste of time. He'd wanted to give the kids some-thing tangible to preserve the already fading mem-ory of their father. But that prettied-up bungalow had nothing to do with Danny and him and the life they'd lived.

At the café, the kids ordered toasted bagels with peanut butter and jam. Mick stuck with coffee, his beverage of choice since Kelly had left him last night. Not that the caffeine helped the throbbing in his head.

He'd been such a bastard, lashing out at her that

way. His breeding—or lack thereof—had really shown through, hadn't it. Her conclusion—that he hated her for shooting Danny—was justifiable. But dead wrong.

He hated *himself.* For having failed Danny when they were younger. For being alive, when Danny was dead. And for having the children, when Danny would never see them again.

"Why didn't Kelly take us with her to see the horses?" Billy asked. His feet dangled from the end of the chair, weighted down with his new cowboy boots.

"I'm not sure." Kelly had phoned this morning, not wanting the children to feel that she'd abandoned them. She'd told them she was at her sister's place for a visit and assured them she'd be home the next day.

He'd heard every word on the extension, and felt guilty about listening in. But it had seemed the safest way to find out about her plans. He couldn't ask to speak with her. Words didn't exist for the apology he owed her. Yet he was going to have to think of something, eventually.

Like admitting I love her.

Turned out he was capable after all. In the space of a few months his life, his heart, his soul had all become centered around Kelly. The prospect of a day without her was hard enough; a lifetime seemed unbearable.

She might come back to him. But if she did, it would be because of the children. And that wasn't good enough. Not anymore.

Options? He didn't see any. He would have to let her go.

"IT'S BEEN FOUR MONTHS since our last session, and I'm even more messed up than before." Kelly made the admission while staring out the window at the trees, which was easier than facing Scott Martin, who was certain to be disappointed with her.

"Lots has happened, hasn't it. You married. You took on the raising of two children."

Funny, but Scott sounded sympathetic, not at all judgmental. She risked a sideways glance. In his gray wool sweater and corduroy pants, Scott was the very antithesis of acrimonious.

"I know what you must think. I was crazy to marry Mick just so I could look after Danny's kids."

"If that was all there was to it, then yeah, I guess it would seem a little far-out."

But that wasn't all there was to it. She hadn't called the way she felt for Mick love at first, but that was what it had turned out to be.

Kelly reached for the bowl of sweets in the center of the coffee table and snagged a peppermint. Scott let the silence drag. Finally, he stood to refill his coffee mug.

"Kelly, why do you think you came to see me today?"

"To make my sisters happy." Maureen had driven up to the B and B Sunday morning. The three sisters and Poppy had had breakfast together and a long talk.

First, they'd hashed over Poppy's revelation. Apparently, their father hadn't told her she had grandchildren. She'd found out when sorting through his personal belongings after his fatal car accident two years ago.

Their father was dead. They had a grandmother—a woman who longed to be an integral part of their lives. These were facts the Shannon sisters had to adjust to.

But Kelly had even more pressing issues to resolve first. Which was why both her sisters had ganged up on her, until she'd finally relented and called the after-hours number on Scott's card.

"Really?" Scott didn't sound impressed. "And why were they so eager for you to talk to me?"

Kelly brushed her hand over the fabric of her jeans. "They think I've been using Mick and the kids as a distraction."

"To avoid dealing with your feelings about the shooting?"

She nodded. "They think that I'm only with Mick and Billy and Amanda because I feel guilty."

"Do you?"

"Of course," she began, then hesitated. For some reason she found herself remembering her confrontation with Sharon in the hospital. "Actually," she amended, "the word that best describes how I feel is *responsible*."

"For what happened to Danny?"

Kelly pushed her hair back from her face, pondering. It was important that she explain this in just the right way. "For the way I dealt with the situation I encountered when I showed up at the ranch that morning. I believe Danny has to take his share of responsibility for his fate."

"Bravo, Kelly," Scott said softly. "And how does this new perspective affect the way you feel about going back to work?"

"I want to do it, Scott. I want to go back." It was true. Saturday night she'd argued the point with Mick out of stubbornness. But she hadn't been absolutely sure until this moment.

"You and I both know the situation you faced with Danny is extremely rare for most RCMP officers. But if you had to deal with a similar scenario...?"

"The possibility frightens me," Kelly admitted. "I don't want to make life-and-death decisions. But neither do I want to live in a society where no one is prepared to step in and stop people like Danny Mizzoni. I mean, picking up a gun and threatening an innocent person the way he did Cathleen—we just can't stand for that.''

Kelly paused for breath, and was struck by Scott's smile. It had stretched into a grin, and she knew she'd gotten carried away.

"I guess I haven't lost the passion after all.''

Scott grew serious. "Don't be embarrassed. Kelly, you have an excellent work record and a promising future ahead of you. Would you believe that the very first day you walked into my office I predicted you'd eventually return to duty?''

She wanted to say no but, facing the sincerity in his eyes, knew he spoke the truth. "How…?''

"I've worked with enough police officers that I can tell when someone has the calling. Kelly, the reason you're so great at your job is that you truly believe in the principles behind what you do.''

Kelly thought he was embellishing her abilities. But she had to admit he was right about police work being her calling. Which led directly to her next problem.

"Mick isn't going to be happy. He doesn't want me returning to the detachment.''

"Do you know why?''

"It'll just be a constant reminder, won't it—that I shot his brother.''

"Maybe. Maybe not. Kelly, it sounds to me as if you and Mick have a lot you need to talk about.''

Kelly agreed. And yet, she was afraid. She'd

promised the kids she'd return home today, but she was totally uncertain of the reception she'd get from Mick.

What if he asked for a divorce? What would she do then?

KELLY CAME BACK, as promised, on Monday at lunchtime. She took over with the kids so he could put in a half day at work. Having her there when he arrived home was a bittersweet joy. Kelly brought a special glow to the house, one he knew he'd never replace—neither in his heart, nor in the children's.

They had pasta for dinner. The kids' favorite. Kelly served all their favorites, including magical salad dressing and anti-potion milk. Amanda and Billy had a carrot-crunching contest.

Mick found he had no appetite. He couldn't relax with the paper, either, after the children's baths. Instead, he tidied and cleaned, started a fire in the living room, put on a pot of coffee.

At eight-thirty he picked up a birch log from the basket on the hearth, then carefully added it to the embers of the fire. Just killing time, waiting for Kelly to join him.

Amanda was already asleep, but tonight, for the first time, Billy had requested that Kelly tuck him in, too.

A development that was as ironic as it was painful. Mick dreaded to think of how the kids would react when they found out Kelly was leaving for good. The possibility for long-term psychological damage was the very reason he'd insisted on this marriage in the first place. What a terribly misguided plan that had turned out to be.

"Seems like all our important conversations happen in this room."

He wheeled at the sound of her voice. In her jeans and bright blue sweatshirt, with her hair pulled back in a ponytail like that, she looked so young and fresh. "Billy finally fell asleep?"

She nodded. "Mick, I want you to know I've made my decision."

His back stiffened, and he reached for the mantel to ground himself. He'd wanted to be the first, the one to make the offer, to be gracious, but she was obviously in a hurry to get this over with.

"I won't contest it," he said.

"*Contest* it? That's an interesting choice of word. Unless..." The pink glow on her cheeks faded. "Are you talking about a divorce?"

"Of course." A blinding thought struck him. "Weren't you?"

She shook her head. "I was referring to my decision to go back to work. I phoned Springer this afternoon. It's all but official..." She stuck her hands in her pockets and tilted her head. "A divorce, Mick? Is that what you want?"

"After the other night, it seemed indicated." God,

his words were coming out so stiff. He brushed back his hair with one hand and realized his palm was damp with perspiration. He couldn't remember the last time he'd felt this nervous.

"About that argument—Mick, do you remember the promises we made when we decided to get married?"

He nodded.

"This was to be a real marriage. We would always be here for the children..."

He nodded again. Yes, they'd had good intentions, and at first they'd done just fine. But the rotten foundation to their relationship had eventually shown through. Kelly was here because of guilt. And he was a bastard for having taken advantage of that.

"We made a mistake," he said. "*I* made a mistake. But don't think I'll hold you to your promises. You're free, Kelly."

She put a hand to her mouth. "Do you hate me that much, then?"

The idea that she could think he hated her was so ridiculous. Then he remembered. He'd as good as told her so, hadn't he? "Kelly, I'm sorry for what I said the other night. I wanted to be angry at you, but it was really myself I blamed. I'm the one who's responsible for the way Danny's life turned out."

He went to the blinds and adjusted them until the

slats were flattened shut. For once he needed no distractions from outside.

"When I was sixteen, I was just like Danny. Drinking, drugs, crime—I wasn't above any of it. Only Harvey Tomchuk's interest in my future changed the course of my destiny. But I wasn't able to change a thing for my brother."

Kelly crossed the room to take his hands. The compassion in her expression made him turn away.

"Mick, you couldn't change Sharon, either, but you tried to help both of them. That's all anyone could ask of you."

She had a generous heart. It was one of the things he most admired about her. Which was why it wasn't right for him to take advantage of her anymore. "What about you, Kelly? How much should I be asking of you?"

"I don't get what you mean…"

"You entered into this marriage to pay for a wrong you didn't commit. Danny and Sharon let their children down, not you. It's not your responsibility to pick up the pieces. It's mine. And I can do it."

"Mick, I don't get it. If you don't hate me for what happened to Danny…"

"Hate you? God, Kelly. Never."

Her eyes rounded to their full almond shape. "Then, why do you want me to go?"

Hadn't he explained? Wasn't she listening? He moved impatiently, but she kept a grip on his hands.

"Why do you want me to go?" she asked again.

Mick tried to stay calm. She was forcing it all out of him. The whole damn confession. Well, he'd let her have it, then. He'd choke out the words. It wouldn't be that hard....

"I fell in love with you, Kelly. That's not your fault. It's no more reason for you to stay in this marriage than your perceived—"

"Could you repeat that first part, please?"

Mick flinched. She didn't know what she was asking. He'd never, *never* spoken those words to another adult. Choking them out again took a real physical effort. "I said that I love you."

"You look so defiant. Mick, love isn't something to be ashamed of."

"I'm not ashamed." He found himself focusing on the company logo etched into the fabric of her shirt. The small block letters were embroidered in the same blue color and were almost unnoticeable.

"Oh, Mick." She pulled him closer, then wound her arms around his neck.

He felt confused. Why was she doing this? He didn't want her sympathy, and yet he couldn't seem to push her away.

"Mick, have you any idea how crazy I am about you? Almost from the very start of our marriage."

This was impossible. He couldn't be hearing

right. He reached one hand to the floppy end of her ponytail. This lovely, perfect woman represented everything he'd thought he could never have. That she would consider whatever feelings she had for him crazy, he perfectly understood.

"Mick, I love you, too."

She didn't mean it. Yet he'd never had reason to doubt Kelly's sincerity in anything she said or did.

"This can't be real."

"Why not? Mick, you're the most amazing man I've ever met. When I'm done with you, you're going to believe it, too."

She turned her face up to his, and he wanted to kiss her. But he was afraid to break the spell. He stared into her eyes, into their deepest, darkest centers, and finally saw that it was true. *She loved him.* A weightless euphoria lifted up the corners of his mouth and curled his toes.

He moved his head slightly, catching her mouth with his, and then stepped back. Love. The idea of it would take some getting used to. He kissed her again, more passionately, almost groaning when she pulled away and placed a finger to his lips.

"One thing, Mick. Are you okay with me returning to work?"

He took a steadying breath. "I'd rather see you doing something safer. But it's your call." He stroked her face, looking forward to stroking every square inch of her later. Soon.

"We're going to be okay, aren't we?" she said. "You and me. Billy and Amanda."

He understood her need for reassurance. They'd traveled such a tortuous route to being a family. It was hard to believe they'd finally arrived.

But they had. Sharon was out of the picture—at least for now. And Billy and Amanda were happy and healthy. Most amazing of all, he'd found a woman who brought him such joy he felt like an entirely new man.

"Yes. Everything's going to be okay," he told his wife softly. And the best part was, he believed every word.

EMERGENCY!

The Family Doctor
by Bobby Hutchinson

**The next Superromance novel in this dramatic
series—set in and around St. Joseph's Hospital
in Vancouver, British Colombia.**

Chief of staff Antony O'Connor has family problems.
His mother is furious at his father for leaving her many
years ago, and now he's coming to visit—with the
woman he loves. Tony's family is taking sides. Patient
care advocate Kate Lewis is an expert at defusing
anger, so she might be able to help him out. With this
problem, at least. Sorting out her feelings for Tony—
and his feelings for her—is about to get trickier!

**Heartwarming stories with a sense of humor,
genuine charm and emotion and lots of family!**

On sale starting April 2002

Available wherever Harlequin books are sold.

HARLEQUIN®
Makes any time special ®

Visit us at www.eHarlequin.com

HSRE

The Shannon Sisters

A Trilogy by C.J. Carmichael
The stories of three sisters from Alberta whose lives and loves are as rocky—and grand—as the mountains they grew up in.

A Second-Chance Proposal
A murder, a bride-to-be left at the altar, a reunion. Is Cathleen Shannon willing to take a second chance on the man involved in these?

A Convenient Proposal
Kelly Shannon feels guilty about what she's done, and Mick Mizzoni feels that he's his brother's keeper—a volatile situation, but maybe one with a convenient way out!

A Lasting Proposal
Maureen Shannon doesn't want risks in her life anymore. Not after everything she's lived through. But Jake Hartman might be proposing a sure thing....

On sale starting February 2002

Available wherever Harlequin books are sold.

HARLEQUIN®
Makes any time special ®